THE
MOUNTAINS

I0616818

STEWART EDWARD WHITE

The Mountains

Stewart Edward White

© 1st World Library – Literary Society, 2005
PO Box 2211
Fairfield, IA 52556
www.1stworldlibrary.org
First Edition

LCCN: 2004195676

Softcover ISBN: 1-4218-0491-3
Hardcover ISBN: 1-4218-0391-7
eBook ISBN: 1-4218-0591-X

Purchase *"The Mountains"*
as a traditional bound book at:
www.1stWorldLibrary.org/purchase.asp?ISBN=1-4218-0491-3

1st World Library Literary Society is a nonprofit
organization dedicated to promoting literacy by:

- Creating a free internet library accessible from any computer worldwide.
- Hosting writing competitions and offering book publishing scholarships.

The Mountains
contributed by Tim, Ed & Rodney
in support of
1st World Library Literary Society

CONTENTS

PREFACE 7

I. THE RIDGE TRAIL 9

II. ON EQUIPMENT 13

III. ON HORSES 22

IV. ON HOW TO GO ABOUT IT 38

V. THE COAST RANGES 47

VI. THE INFERNO 57

VII. THE FOOT-HILLS 64

VIII. THE PINES 68

IX. THE TRAIL 74

X. ON SEEING DEER 88

XI. ON TENDERFEET 97

XII. THE CANON 107

XIII. TROUT, BUCKSKIN, AND PROSPECTORS 116

XIV. ON CAMP COOKERY 130

XV. ON THE WIND AT NIGHT 143

XVI. THE VALLEY 147

XVII. THE MAIN CREST 157

XVIII. THE GIANT FOREST 167

XIX. ON COWBOYS 171

XX. THE GOLDEN TROUT 185

XXI. ON GOING OUT 190

XXII. THE LURE OF THE TRAIL 202

PREFACE

The author has followed a true sequence of events practically in all particulars save in respect to the character of the Tenderfoot. He is in one sense fictitious; in another sense real. He is real in that he is the apotheosis of many tenderfeet, and that everything he does in this narrative he has done at one time or another in the author's experience. He is fictitious in the sense that he is in no way to be identified with the third member of our party in the actual trip.

I

THE RIDGE TRAIL

Six trails lead to the main ridge. They are all good trails, so that even the casual tourist in the little Spanish-American town on the seacoast need have nothing to fear from the ascent. In some spots they contract to an arm's length of space, outside of which limit they drop sheer away; elsewhere they stand up on end, zigzag in lacets each more hair-raising than the last, or fill to demoralization with loose boulders and shale. A fall on the part of your horse would mean a more than serious accident; but Western horses do not fall. The major premise stands: even the casual tourist has no real reason for fear, however scared he may become.

Our favorite route to the main ridge was by a way called the Cold Spring Trail. We used to enjoy taking visitors up it, mainly because you come on the top suddenly, without warning. Then we collected remarks. Everybody, even the most stolid, said something.

You rode three miles on the flat, two in the leafy and gradually ascending creek-bed of a canon, a half hour of laboring steepness in the overarching mountain lilac and laurel. There you came to a great rock gateway which seemed the top of the world. At the gateway was a Bad Place where the ponies planted warily their little hoofs, and the visitor played "eyes front," and besought that his mount should not stumble.

Beyond the gateway a lush level canon into which you plunged as into a bath; then again the laboring trail, up and always up toward the blue California sky, out of the lilacs, and laurels, and redwood chaparral into the manzanita, the Spanish bayonet, the creamy yucca, and the fine angular shale of the upper regions. Beyond the apparent summit you found always other summits yet to be climbed. And all at once, like thrusting your shoulders out of a hatchway, you looked over the top.

Then came the remarks. Some swore softly; some uttered appreciative ejaculation; some shouted aloud; some gasped; one man uttered three times the word "Oh," - once breathlessly, Oh! once in awakening appreciation, OH! once in wild enthusiasm, OH! Then invariably they fell silent and looked.

For the ridge, ascending from seaward in a gradual coquetry of foot-hills, broad low ranges, cross-systems, canons, little flats, and gentle ravines, inland dropped off almost sheer to the river below. And from under your very feet rose, range after range, tier after tier, rank after rank, in increasing crescendo of wonderful tinted mountains to the main crest of the Coast Ranges, the blue distance, the mightiness of California's western systems. The eye followed them up and up, and farther and farther, with the accumulating emotion of a wild rush on a toboggan. There came a point where the fact grew to be almost too big for the appreciation, just as beyond a certain point speed seems to become unbearable. It left you breathless, wonder-stricken, awed. You could do nothing but look, and look, and look again, tongue-tied by the impossibility of doing justice to what you felt. And in the far distance, finally, your soul, grown big in a moment, came to rest on the great precipices and pines of the greatest mountains of all, close under the sky.

In a little, after the change had come to you, a change definite and enduring, which left your inner processes forever different from what they had been, you turned sharp to the west and rode five miles along the knife-edge Ridge Trail to where Rattlesnake Canon led you down and back to your accustomed environment.

To the left as you rode you saw, far on the horizon, rising to the height of your eye, the mountains of the channel islands. Then the deep sapphire of the Pacific, fringed with the soft, unchanging white of the surf and the yellow of the shore. Then the town like a little map, and the lush greens of the wide meadows, the fruit-groves, the lesser ranges - all vivid, fertile, brilliant, and pulsating with vitality. You filled your senses with it, steeped them in the beauty of it. And at once, by a mere turn of the eyes, from the almost crude insistence of the bright primary color of life, you faced the tenuous azures of distance, the delicate mauves and amethysts, the lilacs and saffrons of the arid country.

This was the wonder we never tired of seeing for ourselves, of showing to others. And often, academically, perhaps a little wistfully, as one talks of something to be dreamed of but never enjoyed, we spoke of how fine it would be to ride down into that land of mystery and enchantment, to penetrate one after another the canons dimly outlined in the shadows cast by the westering sun, to cross the mountains lying outspread in easy grasp of the eye, to gain the distant blue Ridge, and see with our own eyes what lay beyond.

For to its other attractions the prospect added that of impossibility, of unattainableness. These rides of ours were day rides. We had to get home by nightfall. Our horses had to be fed, ourselves to be housed. We had not time to continue on down the other side whither the trail led. At the very and literal brink of achievement we were forced to turn back.

Gradually the idea possessed us. We promised ourselves that some day we would explore. In our after-dinner smokes we spoke of it. Occasionally, from some hunter or forest-ranger, we gained little items of information, we learned the fascination of musical names - Mono Canon, Patrera Don Victor, Lloma Paloma, Patrera Madulce, Cuyamas, became familiar to us as syllables. We desired mightily to body them forth to ourselves as facts. The extent of our mental vision expanded. We heard of other mountains far beyond these farthest - mountains whose almost unexplored vastnesses contained great forests, mighty valleys, strong water-courses, beautiful hanging-meadows, deep canons of granite, eternal snows, - mountains so extended, so wonderful, that their secrets offered whole summers of solitary exploration. We came to feel their marvel, we came to respect the inferno of the Desert that hemmed them in. Shortly we graduated from the indefiniteness of railroad maps to the intricacies of geological survey charts. The fever was on us. We must go.

A dozen of us desired. Three of us went; and of the manner of our going, and what you must know who would do likewise, I shall try here to tell.

II

ON EQUIPMENT

If you would travel far in the great mountains where the trails are few and bad, you will need a certain unique experience and skill. Before you dare venture forth without a guide, you must be able to do a number of things, and to do them well.

First and foremost of all, you must be possessed of that strange sixth sense best described as the sense of direction. By it you always know about where you are. It is to some degree a memory for back-tracks and landmarks, but to a greater extent an instinct for the lay of the country, for relative bearings, by which you are able to make your way across-lots back to your starting-place. It is not an uncommon faculty, yet some lack it utterly. If you are one of the latter class, do not venture, for you will get lost as sure as shooting, and being lost in the mountains is no joke.

Some men possess it; others do not. The distinction seems to be almost arbitrary. It can be largely developed, but only in those with whom original endowment of the faculty makes development possible. No matter how long a direction-blind man frequents the wilderness, he is never sure of himself. Nor is the lack any reflection on the intelligence. I once traveled in the

Black Hills with a young fellow who himself frankly confessed that after much experiment he had come to the conclusion he could not "find himself." He asked me to keep near him, and this I did as well as I could; but even then, three times during the course of ten days he lost himself completely in the tumultuous upheavals and canons of that badly mixed region. Another, an old grouse-hunter, walked twice in a circle within the confines of a thick swamp about two miles square. On the other hand, many exhibit almost marvelous skill in striking a bee-line for their objective point, and can always tell you, even after an engrossing and wandering hunt, exactly where camp lies. And I know nothing more discouraging than to look up after a long hard day to find your landmarks changed in appearance, your choice widened to at least five diverging and similar canons, your pockets empty of food, and the chill mountain twilight descending.

Analogous to this is the ability to follow a dim trail. A trail in the mountains often means merely a way through, a route picked out by some prospector, and followed since at long intervals by chance travelers.

It may, moreover, mean the only way through. Missing it will bring you to ever-narrowing ledges, until at last you end at a precipice, and there is no room to turn your horses around for the return. Some of the great box canons thousands of feet deep are practicable by but one passage, - and that steep and ingenious in its utilization of ledges, crevices, little ravines, and "hog's-backs"; and when the only indications to follow consist of the dim vestiges left by your last predecessor, perhaps years before, the affair becomes one of considerable skill and experience. You must be able to pick out scratches made by shod hoofs on the granite, depressions almost filled in by the subsequent fall of decayed vegetation, excoriations on fallen trees. You must have the sense to know AT ONCE when you have overrun these indications, and the patience to turn back immediately to your last certainty, there to pick up the next clue, even if it should take you the rest of the day. In short, it is absolutely necessary that you be at least a persistent tracker.

Parenthetically; having found the trail, be charitable. Blaze it, if there are trees; otherwise "monument" it by piling rocks on top of one another. Thus will those who come after bless your unknown shade.

Third, you must know horses. I do not mean that you should be a horse-show man, with a knowledge of points and pedigrees. But you must learn exactly what they can and cannot do in the matters of carrying weights, making distance, enduring without deterioration hard climbs in high altitudes; what they can or cannot get over in the way of bad places. This last is not always a matter of appearance merely. Some bits of trail, seeming impassable to anything but a goat, a Western horse will negotiate easily; while others, not particularly terrifying in appearance, offer complications of abrupt turn or a single bit of unstable, leg-breaking footing which renders them exceedingly dangerous. You must, moreover, be able to manage your animals to the best advantage in such bad places. Of course you must in the beginning have been wise as to the selection of the horses.

Fourth, you must know good horse-feed when you see it. Your animals are depending entirely on the country; for of course you are carrying no dry feed for them. Their pasturage will present itself under a variety of aspects, all of which you must recognize with certainty. Some of the greenest, lushest, most satisfying-looking meadows grow nothing but water-grasses of large bulk but small nutrition; while apparently barren tracts often conceal small but strong growths of great value. You must differentiate these.

Fifth, you must possess the ability to pare a hoof, fit a shoe cold, nail it in place. A bare hoof does not last long on the granite, and you are far from the nearest blacksmith. Directly in line with this, you must have the trick of picking up and holding a hoof without being kicked, and you must be able to throw and tie without injuring him any horse that declines to be shod in any other way.

Last, you must of course be able to pack a horse well, and must know four or five of the most essential pack-"hitches."

With this personal equipment you ought to be able to get through the country. It comprises the absolutely essential.

But further, for the sake of the highest efficiency, you should add, as finish to your mountaineer's education, certain other items. A knowledge of the habits of deer and the ability to catch trout with fair certainty are almost a necessity when far from the base of supplies. Occasionally the trail goes to pieces entirely: there you must know something of the handling of an axe and pick. Learn how to swim a horse. You will have to take lessons in camp-fire cookery. Otherwise employ a guide. Of course your lungs, heart, and legs must be in good condition.

.

As to outfit, certain especial conditions will differentiate your needs from those of forest and canoe travel.

You will in the changing altitudes be exposed to greater variations in temperature. At morning you may travel in the hot arid foot-hills; at noon you will be in the cool shades of the big pines; towards evening you may wallow through snowdrifts; and at dark you may camp where morning will show you icicles hanging from the brinks of little waterfalls. Behind your saddle you will want to carry a sweater, or better still a buckskin waistcoat. Your arms are never cold anyway, and the pockets of such a waistcoat, made many and deep, are handy receptacles for smokables, matches, cartridges, and the like. For the night-time, when the cold creeps down from the high peaks, you should provide yourself with a suit of very heavy underwear and an extra sweater or a buckskin shirt. The latter is lighter, softer, and more impervious to the wind than the sweater. Here again I wish to place myself on record as opposed to a coat. It is a useless ornament, assumed but rarely, and then only as substitute for a handier garment.

Inasmuch as you will be a great deal called on to handle abrading and sometimes frozen ropes, you will want a pair of heavy buckskin gauntlets. An extra pair of stout high-laced boots with small Hungarian hob-nails will come handy. It is marvelous how quickly leather wears out in the downhill friction of granite and shale. I once found the heels of a new pair of shoes almost ground away by a single giant-strides descent of a steep shale-covered thirteen-thousand-foot mountain. Having no others I patched them with hair-covered rawhide and a bit of horseshoe. It sufficed, but was a long and disagreeable job which an extra pair would have obviated.

Balsam is practically unknown in the high hills, and the rocks are especially hard. Therefore you will take, in addition to your gray army-blanket, a thick quilt or comforter to save your bones. This, with your saddle-blankets and pads as foundation, should give you ease - if you are tough. Otherwise take a second quilt.

A tarpaulin of heavy canvas 17 x 6 feet goes under you, and can be, if necessary, drawn up to cover your head. We never used a tent. Since you do not have to pack your outfit on your own back, you can, if you choose, include a small pillow. Your other personal belongings are those you would carry into the Forest. I have elsewhere described what they should be.

Now as to the equipment for your horses.

The most important point for yourself is your riding-saddle. The cowboy or military style and seat are the only practicable ones. Perhaps of these two the cowboy saddle is the better, for the simple reason that often in roping or leading a refractory horse, the horn is a great help. For steep-trail work the double cinch is preferable to the single, as it need not be pulled so tight to hold the saddle in place.

Your riding-bridle you will make of an ordinary halter by riveting two snaps to the lower part of the head-piece just above the corners of the horse's mouth. These are snapped into the rings of the bit. At night you unsnap the bit, remove it and the reins, and leave the halter part on the horse. Each animal, riding and packing, has furthermore a short lead-rope attached always to his halter-ring.

Of pack-saddles the ordinary sawbuck tree is by all odds the best, provided it fits. It rarely does. If you can adjust the wood accurately to the anatomy of the individual horse, so that the side pieces bear evenly and smoothly without gouging the withers or chafing the back, you are possessed of the handiest machine made for the purpose. Should individual fitting prove impracticable, get an old LOW California riding-tree and have a blacksmith bolt an upright spike on the cantle. You can hang the loops of the kyacks or alforjas - the sacks slung on either side the horse - from the pommel and this iron spike. Whatever the saddle chosen, it should be supplied with breast-straps, breeching, and two good cinches.

The kyacks or alforjas just mentioned are made either of heavy canvas, or of rawhide shaped square and dried over boxes. After drying, the boxes are removed, leaving the stiff rawhide like small trunks open at the top. I prefer the canvas, for the reason that they can be folded and packed for railroad transportation. If a stiffer receptacle is wanted for miscellaneous loose small articles, you can insert a soap-box inside the canvas. It cannot be denied that the rawhide will stand rougher usage.

Probably the point now of greatest importance is that of saddle-padding. A sore back is the easiest thing in the world to induce, - three hours' chafing will turn the trick, - and once it is done you are in trouble for a month. No precautions or pains are too great to take in assuring your pack-animals against this. On a pinch you will give up cheerfully part of your bedding to the cause. However, two good-quality woolen blankets properly and smoothly folded, a pad made of two ordinary collar-pads sewed parallel by means of canvas strips in such a manner as to lie along both sides of the backbone, a well-fitted saddle, and care in packing will nearly always suffice. I have gone months without having to doctor a single abrasion.

You will furthermore want a pack-cinch and a pack-rope for each horse. The former are of canvas or webbing provided with a ring at one end and a big bolted wooden hook at the other. The latter should be half-inch lines of good quality. Thirty-three feet is enough for packing only; but we usually bought them forty feet long, so they could be used also as picket-ropes. Do not fail to include several extra. They are always fraying out, getting broken, being cut to free a fallen horse, or becoming lost.

Besides the picket-ropes, you will also provide for each horse a pair of strong hobbles. Take them to a harness-maker and have him sew inside each ankle-band a broad strip of soft wash-leather twice the width of the band. This will save much chafing. Some advocate sheepskin with the wool on, but this I have found tends to soak up water or to freeze hard. At least two loud cow-bells with neck-straps are handy to assist you in locating whither the bunch may have strayed during the night. They should be hung on the loose horses most inclined to wander.

Accidents are common in the hills. The repair-kit is normally rather comprehensive. Buy a number of extra latigos, or cinch-straps. Include many copper rivets of all sizes - they are the best quick-repair known for almost everything, from putting together a smashed pack-saddle to cobbling a worn-out boot. Your horse-shoeing outfit should be complete with paring-knife, rasp, nail-set, clippers, hammer, nails, and shoes. The latter will be the malleable soft iron, low-calked "Goodenough," which can be fitted cold. Purchase a dozen front shoes and a dozen and a half hind shoes. The latter wear out faster on the trail. A box or so of hob-nails for your own boots, a waxed end and awl, a whetstone, a file, and a piece of buckskin for strings and patches complete the list.

Thus equipped, with your grub supply, your cooking-utensils, your personal effects, your rifle and your fishing-tackle, you should be able to go anywhere that man and horses can go, entirely self-reliant, independent of the towns.

III

ON HORSES

I really believe that you will find more variation of individual and interesting character in a given number of Western horses than in an equal number of the average men one meets on the street. Their whole education, from the time they run loose on the range until the time when, branded, corralled, broken, and saddled, they pick their way under guidance over a bad piece of trail, tends to develop their self-reliance. They learn to think for themselves.

To begin with two misconceptions, merely by way of clearing the ground: the Western horse is generally designated as a "bronco." The term is considered synonymous of horse or pony. This is not so. A horse is "bronco" when he is ugly or mean or vicious or unbroken. So is a cow "bronco" in the same condition, or a mule, or a burro. Again, from certain Western illustrators and from a few samples, our notion of the cow-pony has become that of a lean, rangy, wiry, thin-necked, scrawny beast. Such may be found. But the average good cow-pony is apt to be an exceedingly handsome animal, clean-built, graceful. This is natural, when you stop to think of it, for he is descended direct from Moorish and Arabian stock.

Certain characteristics he possesses beyond the capabilities of the ordinary horse. The most marvelous to me of these is his sure-footedness. Let me give you a few examples.

I once was engaged with a crew of cowboys in rounding up mustangs in southern Arizona. We would ride slowly in through the hills until we caught sight of the herds. Then it was a case of running them down and heading them off, of turning the herd, milling it, of rushing it while confused across country and into the big corrals. The surface of the ground was composed of angular volcanic rocks about the size of your two fists, between which the bunch-grass sprouted. An Eastern rider would ride his horse very gingerly and at a walk, and then thank his lucky stars if he escaped stumbles. The cowboys turned their mounts through at a dead run. It was beautiful to see the ponies go, lifting their feet well up and over, planting them surely and firmly, and nevertheless making speed and attending to the game. Once, when we had pushed the herd up the slope of a butte, it made a break to get through a little hog-back. The only way to head it was down a series of rough boulder ledges laid over a great sheet of volcanic rock. The man at the hog-back put his little gray over the ledges and boulders, down the sheet of rock, - hop, slip, slide, - and along the side hill in time to head off the first of the mustangs. During the ten days of riding I saw no horse fall. The animal I rode, Button by name, never even stumbled.

In the Black Hills years ago I happened to be one of the inmates of a small mining-camp. Each night the work-animals, after being fed, were turned loose in the mountains. As I possessed the only cow-pony in the outfit, he was fed in the corral, and kept up for the purpose of rounding up the others. Every morning one of us used to ride him out after the herd. Often it was necessary to run him at full speed along the mountainside, over rocks, boulders, and ledges, across ravines and gullies. Never but once in three months did he fall.

On the trail, too, they will perform feats little short of marvelous. Mere steepness does not bother them at all. They sit back almost on their haunches, bunch their feet together, and slide. I have seen them go down a hundred feet this way. In rough country they place their feet accurately and quickly, gauge exactly the proper balance. I have led my saddle-horse, Bullet, over country where, undoubtedly to his intense disgust, I myself have fallen a dozen times in the course of a morning. Bullet had no such troubles. Any of the mountain horses will hop cheerfully up or down ledges anywhere. They will even walk a log fifteen or twenty feet above a stream. I have seen the same trick performed in Barnum's circus as a wonderful feat, accompanied by brass bands and breathlessness. We accomplished it on our trip with out any brass bands; I cannot answer for the breathlessness. As for steadiness of nerve, they will walk serenely on the edge of precipices a man would hate to look over, and given a palm's breadth for the soles of their feet, they will get through. Over such a place I should a lot rather trust Bullet than myself.

In an emergency the Western horse is not apt to lose his head. When a pack-horse falls down, he lies still without struggle until eased of his pack and told to get up. If he slips off an edge, he tries to double his fore legs under him and slide. Should he find himself in a tight place, he waits patiently for you to help him, and then proceeds gingerly. A friend of mine rode a horse named Blue. One day, the trail being slippery with rain, he slid and fell. My friend managed a successful jump, but Blue tumbled about thirty feet to the bed of the canon. Fortunately he was not injured. After some difficulty my friend managed to force his way through the chaparral to where Blue stood. Then it was fine to see them. My friend would go ahead a few feet, picking a route. When he had made his decision, he called Blue. Blue came that far, and no farther. Several times the little horse balanced painfully and unsteadily like a goat, all four feet on a boulder, waiting for his signal to advance. In this manner they regained the trail, and proceeded as though nothing had happened. Instances could be multiplied indefinitely.

A good animal adapts himself quickly. He is capable of learning by experience. In a country entirely new to him he soon discovers the best method of getting about, where the feed grows, where he can find water. He is accustomed to foraging for himself. You do not need to show him his pasturage. If there is anything to eat anywhere in the district he will find it. Little tufts of bunch-grass growing concealed under the edges of the brush, he will search out. If he cannot get grass, he knows how to rustle for the browse of small bushes. Bullet would devour sage-brush, when he could get nothing else; and I have even known him philosophically to fill up on dry pine-needles. There is no nutrition in dry pine-needles, but Bullet got a satisfyingly full belly. On the trail a well-seasoned horse will be always on the forage, snatching here a mouthful, yonder a single spear of grass, and all without breaking the regularity of his gait, or delaying the pack-train behind him. At the end of the day's travel he is that much to the good.

By long observation thus you will construct your ideal of the mountain horse, and in your selection of your animals for an expedition you will search always for that ideal. It is only too apt to be modified by personal idiosyncrasies, and proverbially an ideal is difficult of attainment; but you will, with care, come closer to its realization than one accustomed only to the conventionality of an artificially reared horse would believe possible.

The ideal mountain horse, when you come to pick him out, is of medium size. He should be not smaller than fourteen hands nor larger than fifteen. He is strongly but not clumsily built, short-coupled, with none of the snipy speedy range of the valley animal. You will select preferably one of wide full forehead, indicating intelligence, low in the withers, so the saddle will not be apt to gall him. His sureness of foot should be beyond question, and of course he must be an expert at foraging. A horse that knows but one or two kinds of feed, and that starves unless he can find just those kinds, is an abomination. He must not jump when you throw all kinds of rattling and terrifying tarpaulins across him, and he must not mind if the pack-ropes fall about his heels. In the day's march he must follow like a dog without the necessity of a lead-rope, nor must he stray far when turned loose at night.

Fortunately, when removed from the reassuring environment of civilization, horses are gregarious. They hate to be separated from the bunch to which they are accustomed. Occasionally one of us would stop on the trail, for some reason or another, thus dropping behind the pack-train. Instantly the saddle-horse so detained would begin to grow uneasy. Bullet used by all means in his power to try to induce me to proceed. He would nibble me with his lips, paw the ground, dance in a circle, and finally sidle up to me in the position of being mounted, than which he could think of no stronger hint. Then when I had finally remounted, it was hard to hold him in. He would whinny frantically, scramble with enthusiasm up trails steep enough to draw a protest at ordinary times, and rejoin his companions with every symptom of gratification and delight. This gregariousness and alarm at being left alone in a strange country tends to hold them together at night. You are reasonably certain that in the morning, having found one, you will come upon the rest not far away.

The personnel of our own outfit we found most interesting. Although collected from divergent localities they soon became acquainted. In a crowded corral they were always compact in their organization, sticking close together, and resisting as a solid phalanx encroachments on their feed by other and stranger horses. Their internal organization was very amusing. A certain segregation soon took place. Some became leaders; others by common consent were relegated to the position of subordinates.

The order of precedence on the trail was rigidly preserved by the pack-horses. An attempt by Buckshot to pass Dinkey, for example, the latter always met with a bite or a kick by way of hint. If the gelding still persisted, and tried to pass by a long detour, the mare would rush out at him angrily, her ears back, her eyes flashing, her neck extended. And since Buckshot was by no means inclined always to give in meekly, we had opportunities for plenty of amusement. The two were always skirmishing. When by a strategic short cut across the angle of a trail Buckshot succeeded in stealing a march on Dinkey, while she was nipping a mouthful, his triumph was beautiful to see. He never held the place for long, however. Dinkey's was the leadership by force of ambition and energetic character, and at the head of the pack-train she normally marched.

Yet there were hours when utter indifference seemed to fall on the militant spirits. They trailed peacefully and amiably in the rear while Lily or Jenny marched with pride in the coveted advance. But the place was theirs only by sufferance. A bite or a kick sent them back to their own positions when the true leaders grew tired of their vacation.

However rigid this order of precedence, the saddle-animals were acknowledged as privileged; - and knew it. They could go where they pleased. Furthermore theirs was the duty of correcting infractions of the trail discipline, such as grazing on the march, or attempting unauthorized short cuts. They appreciated this duty. Bullet always became vastly indignant if one of the pack-horses misbehaved. He would run at the offender angrily, hustle him to his place with savage nips of his teeth, and drop back to his own position with a comical air of virtue. Once in a great while it would happen that on my spurring up from the rear of the column I would be mistaken for one of the pack-horses attempting illegally to get ahead. Immediately Dinkey or Buckshot would snake his head out crossly to turn me to the rear. It was really ridiculous to see the expression of apology with which they would take it all back, and the ostentatious, nose-elevated indifference in Bullet's very gait as he marched haughtily by. So rigid did all the animals hold this convention that actually in the San Joaquin Valley Dinkey once attempted to head off a Southern Pacific train. She ran at full speed diagonally toward it, her eyes striking fire, her ears back, her teeth snapping in rage because the locomotive would not keep its place behind her ladyship.

Let me make you acquainted with our outfit.

I rode, as you have gathered, an Arizona pony named Bullet. He was a handsome fellow with a chestnut brown coat, long mane and tail, and a beautiful pair of brown eyes. Wes always called him "Baby." He was in fact the youngster of the party, with all the engaging qualities of youth. I never saw a horse more willing. He wanted to do what you wanted him to; it pleased him, and gave him a warm consciousness of virtue which the least observant could not fail to remark. When leading he walked industriously ahead, setting the pace; when driving, - that is, closing up the rear, - he attended strictly to business. Not for the most luscious bunch of grass that ever grew would he pause even for an instant. Yet in his off hours, when I rode irresponsibly somewhere in the middle, he was a great hand to forage. Few choice morsels escaped him. He confided absolutely in his rider in the matter of bad country, and would tackle anything I would put him at. It seemed that he trusted me not to put him at anything that would hurt him. This was an invaluable trait when an example had to be set to the reluctance of the other horses. He was a great swimmer. Probably the most winning quality of his nature was his extreme friend-liness. He was always wandering into camp to be petted, nibbling me over with his lips, begging to have his forehead rubbed, thrusting his nose under an elbow, and otherwise telling how much he thought of us. Whoever broke him did a good job. I never rode a better-reined horse. A mere indication of the bridle-hand turned him to right or left, and a mere raising of the hand without the slightest pressure on the bit stopped him short. And how well he understood cow-work! Turn him loose after the bunch, and he would do the rest. All I had to do was to stick to him. That in itself was no mean task, for he turned like a flash, and was quick as a cat on his feet. At night I always let him go foot free. He would be there in the morning, and I could always walk directly up to him with the bridle in plain sight in my hand. Even at a feedless camp we once made where we had shot a couple of deer, he did not attempt to wander off in search of pasture, as would most horses. He nosed around unsuccessfully until pitch dark, then came into camp, and with great philosophy stood tail to the fire until morning. I could always jump off anywhere for a shot, without even the necessity of "tying him to the ground," by throwing the reins over his head. He would wait for me, although he was never overfond of firearms.

Nevertheless Bullet had his own sense of dignity. He was literally as gentle as a kitten, but he drew a line. I shall never forget how once, being possessed of a desire to find out whether we could swim our outfit across a certain stretch of the Merced River, I climbed him bareback. He bucked me off so quickly that I never even got settled on his back. Then he gazed at me with sorrow, while, laughing irrepressibly at this unusual assertion of independent ideas, I picked myself out of a wild-rose bush. He did not attempt to run away from me, but stood to be saddled, and plunged boldly into the swift water where I told him to. Merely he thought it disrespectful in me to ride him without his proper harness. He was the pet of the camp.

As near as I could make out, he had but one fault. He was altogether too sensitive about his hind quarters, and would jump like a rabbit if anything touched him there.

Wes rode a horse we called Old Slob. Wes, be it premised, was an interesting companion. He had done everything, - seal-hunting, abalone-gathering, boar-hunting, all kinds of shooting, cow-punching in the rough Coast Ranges, and all other queer and outlandish and picturesque vocations by which a man can make a living. He weighed two hundred and twelve pounds and was the best game shot with a rifle I ever saw.

As you may imagine, Old Slob was a stocky individual. He was built from the ground up. His disposition was quiet, slow, honest. Above all, he gave the impression of vast, very vast experience. Never did he hurry his mental processes, although he was quick enough in his movements if need arose. He quite declined to worry about anything. Consequently, in spite of the fact that he carried by far the heaviest man in the company, he stayed always fat and in good condition. There was something almost pathetic in Old Slob's willingness to go on working, even when more work seemed like an imposition. You could not fail to fall in love with his mild inquiring gentle eyes, and his utter trust in the goodness of human nature. His only fault was an excess of caution. Old Slob was very very experienced. He knew all about trails, and he declined to be hurried over what he considered a bad place. Wes used sometimes to disagree with him as to what constituted a bad place. "Some day you're going to take a tumble, you old fool," Wes used to address him, "if you go on fiddling down steep rocks with your little old monkey work. Why don't you step out?" Only Old

Slob never did take a tumble. He was willing to do anything for you, even to the assuming of a pack. This is considered by a saddle-animal distinctly as a come-down.

The Tenderfoot, by the irony of fate, drew a tenderfoot horse. Tunemah was a big fool gray that was constitutionally rattle-brained. He meant well enough, but he didn't know anything. When he came to a bad place in the trail, he took one good look - and rushed it. Constantly we expected him to come to grief. It wore on the Tenderfoot's nerves. Tunemah was always trying to wander off the trail, trying fool routes of his own invention. If he were sent ahead to set the pace, he lagged and loitered and constantly looked back, worried lest he get too far in advance and so lose the bunch. If put at the rear, he fretted against the bit, trying to push on at a senseless speed. In spite of his extreme anxiety to stay with the train, he would once in a blue moon get a strange idea of wandering off solitary through the mountains, passing good feed, good water, good shelter. We would find him, after a greater or less period of difficult tracking, perched in a silly fashion on some elevation. Heaven knows what his idea was: it certainly was neither search for feed, escape, return whence he came, nor desire for exercise. When we came up with him, he would gaze mildly at us from a foolish vacant eye and follow us peaceably back to camp. Like most weak and silly people, he had occasional stubborn fits when you could beat him to a pulp without persuading him. He was one of the type already mentioned that knows but two or three kinds of feed. As time went on he became thinner and thinner. The other horses prospered, but Tunemah failed. He actually did not know enough to take care of himself; and could not learn. Finally, when about two months out, we traded him at a cow-camp for a little buckskin called Monache.

So much for the saddle-horses. The pack-animals were four.

A study of Dinkey's character and an experience of her characteristics always left me with mingled feelings. At times I was inclined to think her perfection: at other times thirty cents would have been esteemed by me as a liberal offer for her. To enumerate her good points: she was an excellent weight-carrier; took good care of her pack that it never scraped nor bumped; knew all about trails, the possibilities of short cuts, the best way of easing herself downhill; kept fat and healthy in districts where grew next to no feed at all; was past-mistress in the picking of routes through a trailless country. Her endurance was marvelous; her intelligence equally so. In fact too great intelligence perhaps accounted for most of her defects. She thought too much for herself; she made up opinions about people; she speculated on just how far each member of the party, man or beast, would stand imposition, and tried conclusions with each to test the accuracy of her speculations; she obstinately insisted on her own way in going up and down hill, - a way well enough for Dinkey, perhaps, but hazardous to the other less skillful animals who naturally would follow her lead. If she did condescend to do things according to your ideas, it was with a mental reservation. You caught her sardonic eye fixed on you contemptuously. You felt at once that she knew another method, a much better method, with which yours compared most unfavorably. "I'd like to kick you in the stomach," Wes used to say; "you know too much for a horse!"

If one of the horses bucked under the pack, Dinkey deliberately tried to stampede the others - and generally succeeded. She invariably led them off whenever she could escape her picket-rope. In case of trouble of any sort, instead of standing still sensibly, she pretended to be subject to wild-eyed panics. It was all pretense, for when you DID yield to temptation and light into her with the toe of your boot, she subsided into common sense. The spirit of malevolent mischief was hers.

Her performances when she was being packed were ridiculously histrionic. As soon as the saddle was cinched, she spread her legs apart, bracing them firmly as though about to receive the weight of an iron safe. Then as each article of the pack was thrown across her back, she flinched and uttered the most heart-rending groans. We used sometimes to amuse ourselves by adding merely an empty sack, or other article quite without weight. The groans and tremblings of the braced legs were quite as pitiful as though we had piled on a sack of flour. Dinkey, I had forgotten to state, was a white horse, and belonged to Wes.

Jenny also was white and belonged to Wes. Her chief characteristic was her devotion to Dinkey. She worshiped Dinkey, and seconded her enthusiastically. Without near the originality of Dinkey, she was yet a very good and sure pack-horse. The deceiving part about Jenny was her eye. It was baleful with the spirit of evil, - snaky and black, and with green sideways gleams in it. Catching the flash of it, you would forever after avoid getting in range of her heels or teeth. But it was all a delusion. Jenny's disposition was mild and harmless.

The third member of the pack-outfit we bought at an auction sale in rather a peculiar manner. About sixty head of Arizona horses of the C. A. Bar outfit were being sold. Toward the close of the afternoon they brought out a well-built stocky buckskin of first-rate appearance except that his left flank was ornamented with five different brands. The auctioneer called attention to him.

"Here is a first-rate all-round horse," said he. "He is sound; will ride, work, or pack; perfectly broken, mild, and gentle. He would make a first-rate family horse, for he has a kind disposition."

The official rider put a saddle on him to give him a demonstrating turn around the track. Then that mild, gentle, perfectly broken family horse of kind disposition gave about as pretty an exhibition of barbed-wire bucking as you would want to see. Even the auctioneer had to join in the wild shriek of delight that went up from the crowd. He could not get a bid, and I bought the animal in later very cheaply.

As I had suspected, the trouble turned out to be merely exuberance or nervousness before a crowd. He bucked once with me under the saddle; and twice subsequently under a pack, - that was all. Buckshot was the best pack-horse we had. Bar an occasional saunter into the brush when he got tired of the trail, we had no fault to find with him. He carried a heavy pack, was as sure-footed as Bullet, as sagacious on the trail as Dinkey, and he always attended strictly to his own business. Moreover he knew that business thoroughly, knew what should be expected of him, accomplished it well and quietly. His disposition was dignified but lovable. As long as you treated him well, he was as gentle as you could ask. But once let Buckshot get it into his head that he was being imposed on, or once let him see that your temper had betrayed you into striking him when he thought he did not deserve it, and he cut loose vigorously and emphatically with his heels. He declined to be abused.

There remains but Lily. I don't know just how to do justice to Lily - the "Lily maid." We named her that because she looked it. Her color was a pure white, her eye was virginal and silly, her long bang strayed in wanton carelessness across her face and eyes, her expression was foolish, and her legs were long and rangy. She had the general appearance of an overgrown school-girl too big for short dresses and too young for long gowns; - a school-girl named Flossie, or Mamie, or Lily. So we named her that.

At first hers was the attitude of the timid and shrinking tenderfoot. She stood in awe of her companions; she appreciated her lack of experience. Humbly she took the rear; slavishly she copied the other horses; closely she clung to camp. Then in a few weeks, like most tenderfeet, she came to think that her short experience had taught her everything there was to know. She put on airs. She became too cocky and conceited for words.

Everything she did was exaggerated, overdone. She assumed her pack with an air that plainly said, "Just see what a good horse am I!" She started out three seconds before the others in a manner intended to shame their procrastinating ways. Invariably she was the last to rest, and the first to start on again. She climbed over-vigorously, with the manner of conscious rectitude. "Acts like she was trying to get her wages raised," said Wes.

In this manner she wore herself down. If permitted she would have climbed until winded, and then would probably have fallen off somewhere for lack of strength. Where the other horses watched the movements of those ahead, in order that when a halt for rest was called they might stop at an easy place on the trail, Lily would climb on until jammed against the animal immediately preceding her. Thus often she found herself forced to cling desperately to extremely bad footing until the others were ready to proceed. Altogether she was a precious nuisance, that acted busily but without thinking.

Two virtues she did possess. She was a glutton for work; and she could fall far and hard without injuring herself. This was lucky, for she was always falling. Several times we went down to her fully expecting to find her dead or so crippled that she would have to be shot. The loss of a little skin was her only injury. She got to be quite philosophic about it. On losing her balance she would tumble peaceably, and then would lie back with an air of luxury, her eyes closed, while we worked to free her. When we had loosened the pack, Wes would twist her tail. Thereupon she would open one eye inquiringly as though to say, "Hullo! Done already?" Then leisurely she would arise and shake herself.

IV

ON HOW TO GO ABOUT IT

One truth you must learn to accept, believe as a tenet of your faith, and act upon always. It is that your entire welfare depends on the condition of your horses. They must, as a consequence, receive always your first consideration. As long as they have rest and food, you are sure of getting along; as soon as they fail, you are reduced to difficulties. So absolute is this truth that it has passed into an idiom. When a Westerner wants to tell you that he lacks a thing, he informs you he is "afoot" for it. "Give me a fill for my pipe," he begs; "I'm plumb afoot for tobacco."

Consequently you think last of your own comfort. In casting about for a place to spend the night, you look out for good feed. That assured, all else is of slight importance; you make the best of whatever camping facilities may happen to be attached. If necessary you will sleep on granite or in a marsh, walk a mile for firewood or water, if only your animals are well provided for. And on the trail you often will work twice as hard as they merely to save them a little. In whatever I may tell you regarding practical expedients, keep this always in mind.

As to the little details of your daily routine in the

Stewart Edward White

mountains, many are worth setting down, however trivial they may seem. They mark the difference between the greenhorn and the old-timer; but, more important, they mark also the difference between the right and the wrong, the efficient and the inefficient ways of doing things.

In the morning the cook for the day is the first man afoot, usually about half past four. He blows on his fingers, casts malevolent glances at the sleepers, finally builds his fire and starts his meal. Then he takes fiendish delight in kicking out the others. They do not run with glad shouts to plunge into the nearest pool, as most camping fiction would have us believe. Not they. The glad shout and nearest pool can wait until noon when the sun is warm. They, too, blow on their fingers and curse the cook for getting them up so early. All eat breakfast and feel better.

Now the cook smokes in lordly ease. One of the other men washes the dishes, while his companion goes forth to drive in the horses. Washing dishes is bad enough, but fumbling with frozen fingers at stubborn hobble-buckles is worse. At camp the horses are caught, and each is tied near his own saddle and pack.

The saddle-horses are attended to first. Thus they are available for business in case some of the others should make trouble. You will see that your saddle-blankets are perfectly smooth, and so laid that the edges are to the front where they are least likely to roll under or wrinkle. After the saddle is in place, lift it slightly and loosen the blanket along the back bone so it will not draw down tight under the weight of the rider. Next hang your rifle-scabbard under your left leg. It should be slanted along the horse's side at such an angle that neither will the muzzle interfere with the animal's hind leg, nor the butt with your bridle-hand. This angle must be determined by experiment. The loop in front should be attached to the scabbard, so it can be hung over the horn; that behind to the saddle, so the muzzle can be thrust through it. When you come to try this method, you will appreciate its handiness. Besides the rifle, you will carry also your rope, camera, and a sweater or waistcoat for changes in temperature. In your saddle bags are pipe and tobacco, perhaps a chunk of bread, your note-book, and the map - if there is any. Thus your saddle-horse is outfitted. Do not forget your collapsible rubber cup. About your waist you will wear your cartridge-belt with six-shooter and sheath-knife. I use a forty-five caliber belt. By threading a buck skin thong in and out through some of the cartridge loops, their size is sufficiently reduced to hold also the 30-40 rifle cartridges. Thus I carry ammunition for both revolver and rifle in the one belt. The belt should not be buckled tight about your waist, but should hang well down on the hip. This is for two reasons. In the first place, it does not drag so heavily at your anatomy, and falls naturally into position when you are mounted. In the second place, you can jerk your gun out more easily from a loose-hanging holster. Let your knife-sheath be so deep as almost to cover the handle, and the knife of the very best steel procurable. I like a thin blade. If you are a student of animal anatomy, you can skin and quarter a deer with nothing heavier than a pocket-knife.

When you come to saddle the pack-horses, you must exercise even greater care in getting the saddle-blankets smooth and the saddle in place. There is some give and take to a rider; but a pack carries "dead," and gives the poor animal the full handicap of its weight at all times. A rider dismounts in bad or steep places; a pack stays on until the morning's journey is ended. See to it, then, that it is on right.

Each horse should have assigned him a definite and, as nearly as possible, unvarying pack. Thus you will not have to search everywhere for the things you need.

For example, in our own case, Lily was known as the cook-horse. She carried all the kitchen utensils, the fire-irons, the axe, and matches. In addition her alforjas contained a number of little bags in which were small quantities for immediate use of all the different sorts of provisions we had with us. When we made camp we unpacked her near the best place for a fire, and everything was ready for the cook. Jenny was a sort of supply store, for she transported the main stock of the provisions of which Lily's little bags contained samples. Dinkey helped out Jenny, and in addition - since she took such good care of her pack - was intrusted with the fishing-rods, the shot-gun, the medicine-bag, small miscellaneous duffle, and whatever deer or bear meat we happened to have. Buckshot's pack consisted of things not often used, such as all the ammunition, the horse-shoeing outfit, repair-kit, and the like. It was rarely disturbed at all.

These various things were all stowed away in the kyacks or alforjas which hung on either side. They had to be very accurately balanced. The least difference in weight caused one side to sag, and that in turn chafed the saddle-tree against the animal's withers.

So far, so good. Next comes the affair of the top packs. Lay your duffle-bags across the middle of the saddle. Spread the blankets and quilts as evenly as possible.

Cover all with the canvas tarpaulin suitably folded. Everything is now ready for the pack-rope.

The first thing anybody asks you when it is discovered that you know a little something of pack-trains is, "Do you throw the Diamond Hitch?" Now the Diamond is a pretty hitch and a firm one, but it is by no means the fetish some people make of it. They would have you believe that it represents the height of the packer's art; and once having mastered it, they use it religiously for every weight, shape, and size of pack. The truth of the matter is that the style of hitch should be varied according to the use to which it is to be put.

The Diamond is good because it holds firmly, is a great flattener, and is especially adapted to the securing of square boxes. It is celebrated because it is pretty and rather difficult to learn. Also it possesses the advantage for single-handed packing that it can be thrown slack throughout and then tightened, and that the last pull tightens the whole hitch. However, for ordinary purposes, with a quiet horse and a comparatively soft pack, the common Square Hitch holds well enough and is quickly made. For a load of small articles and heavy alforjas there is nothing like the Lone Packer. It too is a bit hard to learn. Chiefly is it valuable because the last pulls draw the alforjas away from the horse's sides, thus preventing their chafing him. Of the many hitches that remain, you need learn, to complete your list for all practical purposes, only the Bucking Hitch. It is complicated, and takes time and patience to throw, but it is warranted to hold your deck-load through the most violent storms bronco ingenuity can stir up.

These four will be enough. Learn to throw them, and take pains always to throw them good and tight. A loose pack is the best expedient the enemy of your soul could possibly devise. It always turns or comes to pieces on the edge of things; and then you will spend the rest of the morning trailing a wildly bucking horse by the burst and scattered articles of camp duffle. It is furthermore your exhilarating task, after you have caught him, to take stock, and spend most of the afternoon looking for what your first search passed by. Wes and I once hunted two hours for as large an object as a Dutch oven. After which you can repack. This time you will snug things down. You should have done so in the beginning.

Next, the lead-ropes are made fast to the top of the packs. There is here to be learned a certain knot. In case of trouble you can reach from your saddle and jerk the whole thing free by a single pull on a loose end.

All is now ready. You take a last look around to see that nothing has been left. One of the horsemen starts on ahead. The pack-horses swing in behind. We soon accustomed ours to recognize the whistling of "Boots and Saddles" as a signal for the advance. Another horseman brings up the rear. The day's journey has begun.

To one used to pleasure-riding the affair seems almost too deliberate. The leader plods steadily, stopping from time to time to rest on the steep slopes. The others string out in a leisurely procession. It does no good to hurry. The horses will of their own accord stay in sight of one another, and constant nagging to keep the rear closed up only worries them without accomplishing any valuable result. In going uphill especially, let the train take its time. Each animal is likely to have his own ideas about when and where to rest. If he does, respect them. See to it merely that there is no prolonged yielding to the temptation of meadow feed, and no careless or malicious straying off the trail. A minute's difference in the time of arrival does not count. Remember that the horses are doing hard and continuous work on a grass diet.

The day's distance will not seem to amount to much in actual miles, especially if, like most Californians, you are accustomed on a fresh horse to make an occasional sixty or seventy between suns; but it ought to suffice. There is a lot to be seen and enjoyed in a mountain mile. Through the high country two miles an hour is a fair average rate of speed, so you can readily calculate that fifteen make a pretty long day. You will be afoot a good share of the time. If you were out from home for only a few hours' jaunt, undoubtedly you would ride your horse over places where in an extended trip you will prefer to lead him. It is always a question of saving your animals.

About ten o'clock you must begin to figure on water. No horse will drink in the cool of the morning, and so, when the sun gets well up, he will be thirsty. Arrange it.

As to the method of travel, you can either stop at noon or push straight on through. We usually arose about half past four; got under way by seven; and then rode continuously until ready to make the next camp. In the high country this meant until two or three in the afternoon, by which time both we and the horses were pretty hungry. But when we did make camp, the horses had until the following morning to get rested and to graze, while we had all the remainder of the afternoon to fish, hunt, or loaf. Sometimes, however, it was more expedient to make a lunch-camp at noon. Then we allowed an hour for grazing, and about half an hour to pack and unpack. It meant steady work for ourselves. To unpack, turn out the horses, cook, wash dishes, saddle up seven animals, and repack, kept us very busy. There remained not much leisure to enjoy the scenery. It freshened the horses, however, which was the main point. I should say the first method was the better for ordinary journeys; and the latter for those times when, to reach good feed, a forced march becomes necessary.

On reaching the night's stopping-place, the cook for the day unpacks the cook-horse and at once sets about the preparation of dinner. The other two attend to the animals. And no matter how tired you are, or how hungry you may be, you must take time to bathe their backs with cold water; to stake the picket-animal where it will at once get good feed and not tangle its rope in bushes, roots, or stumps; to hobble the others; and to bell those inclined to wander. After this is done, it is well, for the peace and well-being of the party, to take food.

A smoke establishes you in the final and normal attitude of good humor. Each man spreads his tarpaulin where he has claimed his bed. Said claim is indicated by his hat thrown down where he wishes to sleep. It is a mark of pre-emption which every one is bound to respect. Lay out your saddle-blankets, cover them with your quilt, place the sleeping-blanket on top, and fold over the tarpaulin to cover the whole. At the head deposit your duffle-bag. Thus are you assured of a pleasant night.

About dusk you straggle in with trout or game. The camp-keeper lays aside his mending or his repairing or his note-book, and stirs up the cooking-fire. The smell of broiling and frying and boiling arises in the air. By the dancing flame of the campfire you eat your third dinner for the day - in the mountains all meals are dinners, and formidable ones at that. The curtain of blackness draws down close. Through it shine stars, loom mountains cold and mist-like in the moon. You tell stories. You smoke pipes. After a time the pleasant chill creeps down from the eternal snows. Some one throws another handful of pine-cones on the fire. Sleepily you prepare for bed. The pine-cones flare up, throwing their light in your eyes. You turn over and wrap the soft woolen blanket close about your chin. You wink drowsily and at once you are asleep. Along late in the night you awaken to find your nose as cold as a dog's. You open one eye. A few coals mark where the fire has been. The mist mountains have drawn nearer, they seem to bend over you in silent contemplation. The moon is sailing high in the heavens.

With a sigh you draw the canvas tarpaulin over your head. Instantly it is morning.

V

THE COAST RANGES

At last, on the day appointed, we, with five horses, climbed the Cold Spring Trail to the ridge; and then, instead of turning to the left, we plunged down the zigzag lacets of the other side. That night we camped at Mono Canon, feeling ourselves strangely an integral part of the relief map we had looked upon so many times that almost we had come to consider its features as in miniature, not capacious for the accommodation of life-sized men. Here we remained a day while we rode the hills in search of Dinkey and Jenny, there pastured.

We found Jenny peaceful and inclined to be corralled. But Dinkey, followed by a slavishly adoring brindle mule, declined to be rounded up. We chased her up hill and down; along creek-beds and through the spiky chaparral. Always she dodged craftily, warily, with forethought. Always the brindled mule, wrapt in admiration at his companion's cleverness, crashed along after. Finally we teased her into a narrow canon. Wes and the Tenderfoot closed the upper end. I attempted to slip by to the lower, but was discovered. Dinkey tore a frantic mile down the side hill. Bullet, his nostrils wide, his ears back, raced parallel in the boulder-strewn stream-bed, wonderful in his avoidance of bad footing, precious in his selection of good, interested in the game, indignant at the wayward Dinkey, profoundly contemptuous of the besotted mule. At a bend in the canon interposed a steep bank. Up this we scrambled, dirt and stones flying. I had just time to bend low along the saddle when, with the ripping and tearing and scratching of thorns, we burst blindly through a thicket. In the open space on the farther side Bullet stopped, panting but triumphant. Dinkey, surrounded at last, turned back toward camp with an air of utmost indifference. The mule dropped his long ears and followed.

At camp we corralled Dinkey, but left her friend to shift for himself. Then was lifted up his voice in mulish lamentations until, cursing, we had to ride out bareback and drive him far into the hills and there stone him into distant fear. Even as we departed up the trail the following day the voice of his sorrow, diminishing like the echo of grief, appealed uselessly to Dinkey's sympathy. For Dinkey, once captured, seemed to have shrugged her shoulders and accepted inevitable toil with a real though cynical philosophy.

The trail rose gradually by imperceptible gradations and occasional climbs. We journeyed in the great canons. High chaparral flanked the trail, occasional wide gray stretches of "old man" filled the air with its pungent odor and with the calls of its quail. The crannies of the rocks, the stretches of wide loose shale, the crumbling bottom earth offered to the eye the dessicated beauties of creamy yucca, of yerba buena, of the gaudy red paint-brushes, the Spanish bayonet; and to the nostrils the hot dry perfumes of the semi-arid lands. The air was tepid; the sun hot. A sing-song of bees and locusts and strange insects lulled the mind.

The ponies plodded on cheerfully. We expanded and basked and slung our legs over the pommels of our saddles and were glad we had come.

At no time did we seem to be climbing mountains. Rather we wound in and out, round and about, through a labyrinth of valleys and canons and ravines, farther and farther into a mysterious shut-in country that seemed to have no end. Once in a while, to be sure, we zigzagged up a trifling ascent; but it was nothing. And then at a certain point the Tenderfoot happened to look back.

"Well!" he gasped; "will you look at that!"

We turned. Through a long straight aisle which chance had placed just there, we saw far in the distance a sheer slate-colored wall; and beyond, still farther in the distance, overtopping the slate-colored wall by a narrow strip, another wall of light azure blue.

"It's our mountains," said Wes, "and that blue ridge is the channel islands. We've got up higher than our range."

We looked about us, and tried to realize that we were actually more than halfway up the formidable ridge we had so often speculated on from the Cold Spring Trail. But it was impossible. In a few moments, however, our broad easy canon narrowed. Huge crags and sheer masses of rock hemmed us in. The chaparral and yucca and yerba buena gave place to pine-trees and mountain oaks, with little close clumps of cottonwoods in the stream bottom. The brook narrowed and leaped, and the white of alkali faded from its banks. We began to climb in good earnest, pausing often for breath. The view opened. We looked back on whence we had come, and saw again, from the reverse, the forty miles of ranges and valleys we had viewed from the Ridge Trail.

At this point we stopped to shoot a rattlesnake. Dinkey and Jenny took the opportunity to push ahead. From time to time we would catch sight of them traveling earnestly on, following the trail accurately, stopping at stated intervals to rest, doing their work, conducting themselves as decorously as though drivers had stood over them with blacksnake whips. We tried a little to catch up.

"Never mind," said Wes, "they've been over this trail before. They'll stop when they get to where we're going to camp."

We halted a moment on the ridge to look back over the lesser mountains and the distant ridge, beyond which the islands now showed plainly. Then we dropped down behind the divide into a cup valley containing a little meadow with running water on two sides of it and big pines above. The meadow was brown, to be sure, as all typical California is at this time of year. But the brown of California and the brown of the East are two different things. Here is no snow or rain to mat down the grass, to suck out of it the vital principles. It grows ripe and sweet and soft, rich with the life that has not drained away, covering the hills and valleys with the effect of beaver fur, so that it seems the great round-backed hills must have in a strange manner the yielding flesh-elasticity of living creatures. The brown of California is the brown of ripeness; not of decay.

Our little meadow was beautifully named Madulce,[1]

Stewart Edward White

and was just below the highest point of this section of the Coast Range. The air drank fresh with the cool of elevation. We went out to shoot supper; and so found ourselves on a little knoll fronting the brown-hazed east. As we stood there, enjoying the breeze after our climb, a great wave of hot air swept by us, filling our lungs with heat, scorching our faces as the breath of a furnace. Thus was brought to our minds what, in the excitement of a new country, we had forgotten, - that we were at last on the eastern slope, and that before us waited the Inferno of the desert.

[1] In all Spanish names the final e should be pronounced.

That evening we lay in the sweet ripe grasses of Madulce, and talked of it. Wes had been across it once before and did not possess much optimism with which to comfort us.

"It's hot, just plain hot," said he, "and that's all there is about it. And there's mighty little water, and what there is is sickish and a long ways apart. And the sun is strong enough to roast potatoes in."

"Why not travel at night?" we asked.

"No place to sleep under daytimes," explained Wes. "It's better to keep traveling and then get a chance for a little sleep in the cool of the night."

We saw the reasonableness of that.

"Of course we'll start early, and take a long nooning, and travel late. We won't get such a lot of sleep."

"How long is it going to take us?"

Wes calculated.

"About eight days," he said soberly.

The next morning we descended from Madulce abruptly by a dirt trail, almost perpendicular until we slid into a canon of sage-brush and quail, of mescale cactus and the fierce dry heat of sun-baked shale.

"Is it any hotter than this on the desert?" we inquired.

Wes looked on us with pity.

"This is plumb arctic," said he.

Near noon we came to a little cattle ranch situated in a flat surrounded by red dikes and buttes after the manner of Arizona. Here we unpacked, early as it was, for through the dry countries one has to apportion his day's journeys by the water to be had. If we went farther to-day, then to-morrow night would find us in a dry camp.

The horses scampered down the flat to search out alfilaria. We roosted under a slanting shed, - where were stock saddles, silver-mounted bits and spurs, rawhide riatas, branding-irons, and all the lumber of the cattle business, - and hung out our tongues and gasped for breath and earnestly desired the sun to go down or a breeze to come up. The breeze shortly did so. It was a hot breeze, and availed merely to cover us with dust, to swirl the stable-yard into our faces. Great swarms of flies buzzed and lit and stung. Wes, disgusted, went over to where a solitary cow-puncher was engaged in shoeing a horse. Shortly we saw Wes pressed into service to hold the horse's hoof. He raised a pathetic face to us, the big round drops chasing each other down it as fast as rain. We grinned and felt better.

The fierce perpendicular rays of the sun beat down. The air under the shed grew stuffier and more oppressive, but it was the only patch of shade in all that pink and red furnace of a little valley. The Tender-foot discovered a pair of horse-clippers, and, becoming slightly foolish with the heat, insisted on our barbering his head. We told him it was cooler with hair than without; and that the flies and sun would be offered thus a beautiful opportunity, but without avail. So we clipped him, - leaving, however, a beautiful long scalp-lock in the middle of his crown. He looked like High-low-kickapoo-waterpot, chief of the Wam-wams. After a while he discovered it, and was unhappy.

Shortly the riders began to come in, jingling up to the shed, with a rattle of spurs and bit-chains. There they unsaddled their horses, after which, with great unanimity, they soused their heads in the horse-trough. The chief, a six-footer, wearing beautifully decorated gauntlets and a pair of white buckskin chaps, went so far as to say it was a little warm for the time of year. In the freshness of evening, when frazzled nerves had regained their steadiness, he returned to smoke and yarn with us and tell us of the peculiarities of the cattle business in the Cuyamas. At present he and his men were riding the great mountains, driving the cattle to the lowlands in anticipation of a rodeo the following week. A rodeo under that sun!

We slept in the ranch vehicles, so the air could get

under us. While the stars still shone, we crawled out, tired and unrefreshed. The Tenderfoot and I went down the valley after the horses. While we looked, the dull pallid gray of dawn filtered into the darkness, and so we saw our animals, out of proportion, monstrous in the half light of that earliest morning. Before the range riders were even astir we had taken up our journey, filching thus a few hours from the inimical sun.

Until ten o'clock we traveled in the valley of the Cuyamas. The river was merely a broad sand and stone bed, although undoubtedly there was water below the surface. California rivers are said to flow bottom up. To the northward were mountains typical of the arid countries, - boldly defined, clear in the edges of their folds, with sharp shadows and hard, uncompromising surfaces. They looked brittle and hollow, as though made of papier mache and set down in the landscape. A long four hours' noon we spent beneath a live-oak near a tiny spring. I tried to hunt, but had to give it up. After that I lay on my back and shot doves as they came to drink at the spring. It was better than walking about, and quite as effective as regards supper. A band of cattle filed stolidly in, drank, and filed as stolidly away. Some half-wild horses came to the edge of the hill, stamped, snorted, essayed a tentative advance. Them we drove away, lest they decoy our own animals. The flies would not let us sleep. Dozens of valley and mountain quail called with maddening cheerfulness and energy. By a mighty exercise of will we got under way again. In an hour we rode out into what seemed to be a grassy foot-hill country, supplied with a most refreshing breeze.

The little round hills of a few hundred feet rolled gently away to the artificial horizon made by their

Stewart Edward White

closing in. The trail meandered white and distinct through the clear fur-like brown of their grasses. Cattle grazed. Here and there grew live-oaks, planted singly as in a park. Beyond we could imagine the great plain, grading insensibly into these little hills.

And then all at once we surmounted a slight elevation, and found that we had been traveling on a plateau, and that these apparent little hills were in reality the peaks of high mountains.

We stood on the brink of a wide smooth velvet-creased range that dipped down and down to miniature canons far below. Not a single little boulder broke the rounded uniformity of the wild grasses. Out from beneath us crept the plain, sluggish and inert with heat.

Threads of trails, dull white patches of alkali, vague brown areas of brush, showed indeterminate for a little distance. But only for a little distance. Almost at once they grew dim, faded in the thickness of atmosphere, lost themselves in the mantle of heat that lay palpable and brown like a shimmering changing veil, hiding the distance in mystery and in dread. It was a land apart; a land to be looked on curiously from the vantage-ground of safety, - as we were looking on it from the shoulder of the mountain, - and then to be turned away from, to be left waiting behind its brown veil for what might come. To abandon the high country, deliberately to cut loose from the known, deliberately to seek the presence that lay in wait, - all at once it seemed the height of grotesque perversity. We wanted to turn on our heels. We wanted to get back to our hills and fresh breezes and clear water, to our beloved cheerful quail, to our trails and the sweet upper air.

For perhaps a quarter of an hour we sat our horses, gazing down. Some unknown disturbance lazily rifted the brown veil by ever so little. We saw, lying inert and languid, obscured by its own rank steam, a great round lake. We knew the water to be bitter, poisonous. The veil drew together again. Wes shook himself and sighed, "There she is, - damn her!" said he.

VI

THE INFERNO

For eight days we did penance, checking off the hours, meeting doggedly one after another the disagreeable things. We were bathed in heat; we inhaled it; it soaked into us until we seemed to radiate it like so many furnaces. A condition of thirst became the normal condition, to be only slightly mitigated by a few mouthfuls from zinc canteens of tepid water. Food had no attractions: even smoking did not taste good. Always the flat country stretched out before us. We could see far ahead a landmark which we would reach only by a morning's travel. Nothing intervened between us and it. After we had looked at it a while, we became possessed of an almost insane necessity to make a run for it. The slow maddening three miles an hour of the pack-train drove us frantic. There were times when it seemed that unless we shifted our gait, unless we stepped outside the slow strain of patience to which the Inferno held us relentlessly, we should lose our minds and run round and round in circles - as people often do, in the desert.

And when the last and most formidable hundred yards had slunk sullenly behind us to insignificance, and we had dared let our minds relax from the insistent need of self-control - then, beyond the cotton. woods, or creek-bed, or group of buildings, whichever it might be, we made out another, remote as paradise, to which we must gain by sunset. So again the wagon-trail, with its white choking dust, its staggering sun, its miles made up of monotonous inches, each clutching for a man's sanity.

We sang everything we knew; we told stories; we rode cross-saddle, sidewise, erect, slouching; we walked and led our horses; we shook the powder of years from old worn jokes, conundrums, and puzzles, - and at the end, in spite of our best efforts, we fell to morose silence and the red-eyed vindictive contemplation of the objective point that would not seem to come nearer.

For now we lost accurate sense of time. At first it had been merely a question of going in at one side of eight days, pressing through them, and coming out on the other side. Then the eight days would be behind us. But once we had entered that enchanted period, we found ourselves more deeply involved. The seemingly limited area spread with startling swiftness to the very horizon. Abruptly it was borne in on us that this was never going to end; just as now for the first time we realized that it had begun infinite ages ago. We were caught in the entanglement of days. The Coast Ranges were the experiences of a past incarnation: the Mountains were a myth.

Nothing was real but this; and this would endure forever. We plodded on because somehow it was part of the great plan that we should do so. Not that it did any good: - we had long since given up such ideas. The illusion was very real; perhaps it was the anodyne mercifully administered to those who pass through

Stewart Edward White

the Inferno.

Most of the time we got on well enough. One day, only, the Desert showed her power. That day, at five of the afternoon, it was one hundred and twenty degrees in the shade. And we, through necessity of reaching the next water, journeyed over the alkali at noon. Then the Desert came close on us and looked us fair in the eyes, concealing nothing. She killed poor Deuce, the beautiful setter who had traveled the wild countries so long; she struck Wes and the Tenderfoot from their horses when finally they had reached a long-legged water tank; she even staggered the horses themselves. And I, lying under a bush where I had stayed after the others in the hope of succoring Deuce, began idly shooting at ghostly jack-rabbits that looked real, but through which the revolver bullets passed without resistance.

After this day the Tenderfoot went water-crazy. Watering the horses became almost a mania with him. He could not bear to pass even a mud-hole without offering the astonished Tunemah a chance to fill up, even though that animal had drunk freely not twenty rods back. As for himself, he embraced every opportunity; and journeyed draped in many canteens.

After that it was not so bad. The thermometer stood from a hundred to a hundred and five or six, to be sure, but we were getting used to it. Discomfort, ordinary physical discomfort, we came to accept as the normal environment of man. It is astonishing how soon uniformly uncomfortable conditions, by very lack of contrast, do lose their power to color the habit of mind. I imagine merely physical unhappiness is a matter more of contrasts than of actual circumstances. We

swallowed dust; we humped our shoulders philosophically under the beating of the sun, we breathed the
debris of high winds; we cooked anyhow, ate anything,
spent long idle fly-infested hours waiting for the noon
to pass; we slept in horse-corrals, in the trail, in the
dust, behind stables, in hay, anywhere. There was little
water, less wood for the cooking.

It is now all confused, an impression of events with out
sequence, a mass of little prominent purposeless things
like rock conglomerate. I remember leaning my elbows
on a low window-ledge and watching a poker game
going on in the room of a dive. The light came from a
sickly suspended lamp. It fell on five players, - two
miners in their shirt-sleeves, a Mexican, a tough youth
with side-tilted derby hat, and a fat gorgeously dressed
Chinaman. The men held their cards close to their
bodies, and wagered in silence. Slowly and regularly
the great drops of sweat gathered on their faces. As
regularly they raised the backs of their hands to wipe
them away. Only the Chinaman, broad-faced, calm,
impassive as Buddha, save for a little crafty smile in
one corner of his eye, seemed utterly unaffected by the
heat, cool as autumn. His loose sleeve fell back from
his forearm when he moved his hand forward, laying
his bets. A jade bracelet slipped back and forth as
smoothly as on yellow ivory.

Or again, one night when the plain was like a sea of
liquid black, and the sky blazed with stars, we rode by
a sheep-herder's camp. The flicker of a fire threw a
glow out into the dark. A tall wagon, a group of
silhouetted men, three or four squatting dogs, were
squarely within the circle of illumination. And outside,
in the penumbra of shifting half light, now showing
clearly, now fading into darkness, were the sheep,

indeterminate in bulk, melting away by mysterious thousands into the mass of night. We passed them. They looked up, squinting their eyes against the dazzle of their fire. The night closed about us again.

Or still another: in the glare of broad noon, after a hot and trying day, a little inn kept by a French couple. And there, in the very middle of the Inferno, was served to us on clean scrubbed tables, a meal such as one gets in rural France, all complete, with the potage, the fish fried in oil, the wonderful ragout, the chicken and salad, the cheese and the black coffee, even the vin ordinaire. I have forgotten the name of the place, its location on the map, the name of its people, - one has little to do with detail in the Inferno, - but that dinner never will I forget, any more than the Tenderfoot will forget his first sight of water the day when the Desert "held us up."

Once the brown veil lifted to the eastward. We, souls struggling, saw great mountains and the whiteness of eternal snow. That noon we crossed a river, hurrying down through the flat plain, and in its current came the body of a drowned bear-cub, an alien from the high country.

These things should have been as signs to our jaded spirits that we were nearly at the end of our penance, but discipline had seared over our souls, and we rode on unknowing.

Then we came on a real indication. It did not amount to much. Merely a dry river-bed; but the farther bank, instead of being flat, cut into a low swell of land. We skirted it. Another swell of land, like the sullen after-heave of a storm, lay in our way. Then we crossed a ravine. It was not much of a ravine; in fact it was more like a slight gouge in the flatness of the country. After that we began to see oak-trees, scattered at rare intervals. So interested were we in them that we did not notice rocks beginning to outcrop through the soil until they had become numerous enough to be a feature of the landscape. The hills, gently, quietly, without abrupt transition, almost as though they feared to awaken our alarm by too abrupt movement of growth, glided from little swells to bigger swells. The oaks gathered closer together. The ravine's brother could almost be called a canon. The character of the country had entirely changed.

And yet, so gradually had this change come about that we did not awaken to a full realization of our escape. To us it was still the plain, a trifle modified by local peculiarity, but presently to resume its wonted aspect. We plodded on dully, anodyned with the desert patience.

But at a little before noon, as we rounded the cheek of a slope, we encountered an errant current of air. It came up to us curiously, touched us each in turn, and went on. The warm furnace heat drew in on us again. But it had been a cool little current of air, with something of the sweetness of pines and water and snow-banks in it. The Tenderfoot suddenly reined in his horse and looked about him.

"Boys!" he cried, a new ring of joy in his voice, "we're in the foot-hills!"

Wes calculated rapidly. "It's the eighth day to-day: I guessed right on the time."

We stretched our arms and looked about us. They were dry brown hills enough; but they were hills, and they had trees on them, and canons in them, so to our eyes, wearied with flatness, they seemed wonderful.

VII

THE FOOT-HILLS

At once our spirits rose. We straightened in our saddles, we breathed deep, we joked. The country was scorched and sterile; the wagon-trail, almost paralleling the mountains themselves on a long easy slant toward the high country, was ankle-deep in dust; the ravines were still dry of water. But it was not the Inferno, and that one fact sufficed. After a while we crossed high above a river which dashed white water against black rocks, and so were happy.

The country went on changing. The change was always imperceptible, as is growth, or the stealthy advance of autumn through the woods. From moment to moment one could detect no alteration. Something intangible was taken away; something impalpable added. At the end of an hour we were in the oaks and sycamores; at the end of two we were in the pines and low mountains of Bret Harte's Forty-Nine.

The wagon-trail felt ever farther and farther into the hills. It had not been used as a stage-route for years, but the freighting kept it deep with dust, that writhed and twisted and crawled lazily knee-high to our horses, like a living creature. We felt the swing and sweep of the route. The boldness of its stretches, the freedom of

Stewart Edward White

its reaches for the opposite slope, the wide curve of its horseshoes, all filled us with the breath of an expansion which as yet the broad low country only suggested.

Everything here was reminiscent of long ago. The very names hinted stories of the Argonauts. Coarse Gold Gulch, Whiskey Creek, Grub Gulch, Fine Gold Post-Office in turn we passed. Occasionally, with a fine round dash into the open, the trail drew one side to a stage-station. The huge stables, the wide corrals, the low living-houses, each shut in its dooryard of blazing riotous flowers, were all familiar. Only lacked the old-fashioned Concord coach, from which to descend Jack Hamlin or Judge Starbottle. As for M'liss, she was there, sunbonnet and all.

Down in the gulch bottoms were the old placer diggings. Elaborate little ditches for the deflection of water, long cradles for the separation of gold, decayed rockers, and shining in the sun the tons and tons of pay dirt which had been turned over pound by pound in the concentrating of its treasure. Some of the old cabins still stood. It was all deserted now, save for the few who kept trail for the freighters, or who tilled the restricted bottom-lands of the flats. Road-runners racked away down the paths; squirrels scurried over worn-out placers; jays screamed and chattered in and out of the abandoned cabins. Strange and shy little creatures and birds, reassured by the silence of many years, had ventured to take to themselves the engines of man's industry. And the warm California sun embalmed it all in a peaceful forgetfulness.

Now the trees grew bigger, and the hills more impressive. We should call them mountains in the

East. Pines covered them to the top, straight slender pines with voices. The little flats were planted with great oaks. When we rode through them, they shut out the hills, so that we might have imagined ourselves in the level wooded country. There insisted the effect of limitless tree-grown plains, which the warm drowsy sun, the park-like landscape, corroborated. And yet the contrast of the clear atmosphere and the sharp air equally insisted on the mountains. It was a strange and delicious double effect, a contradiction of natural impressions, a negation of our right to generalize from previous experience.

Always the trail wound up and up. Never was it steep; never did it command an outlook. Yet we felt that at last we were rising, were leaving the level of the Inferno, were nearing the threshold of the high country.

Mountain peoples came to the edges of their clearings and gazed at us, responding solemnly to our salutations. They dwelt in cabins and held to agriculture and the herding of the wild mountain cattle. From them we heard of the high country to which we were bound. They spoke of it as you or I would speak of interior Africa, as something inconceivably remote, to be visited only by the adventurous, an uninhabited realm of vast magnitude and unknown dangers. In the same way they spoke of the plains. Only the narrow pine-clad strip between the two and six thousand feet of elevation they felt to be their natural environment. In it they found the proper conditions for their existence. Out of it those conditions lacked. They were as much a localized product as are certain plants which occur only at certain altitudes. Also were they densely ignorant of trails and routes outside of their own little districts.

All this, you will understand, was in what is known as the low country. The landscape was still brown; the streams but trickles; sage-brush clung to the ravines; the valley quail whistled on the side hills.

But one day we came suddenly into the big pines and rocks; and that very night we made our first camp in a meadow typical of the mountains we had dreamed about.

VIII

THE PINES

I do not know exactly how to make you feel the charm of that first camp in the big country. Certainly I can never quite repeat it in my own experience.

Remember that for two months we had grown accustomed to the brown of the California landscape, and that for over a week we had traveled in the Inferno. We had forgotten the look of green grass, of abundant water; almost had we forgotten the taste of cool air. So invariably had the trails been dusty, and the camping-places hard and exposed, that we had come subconsciously to think of such as typical of the country. Try to put yourself in the frame of mind those conditions would make.

Then imagine yourself climbing in an hour or so up into a high ridge country of broad cup-like sweeps and bold outcropping ledges. Imagine a forest of pine-trees bigger than any pines you ever saw before, - pines eight and ten feet through, so huge that you can hardly look over one of their prostrate trunks even from the back of your pony. Imagine, further, singing little streams of ice-cold water, deep refreshing shadows, a soft carpet of pine-needles through which the faint furrow of the trail runs as over velvet. And then, last of all, in a wide opening, clear as though chopped and plowed by some back-woodsman, a park of grass, fresh grass, green as a precious stone.

This was our first sight of the mountain meadows. From time to time we found others, sometimes a half dozen in a day. The rough country came down close about them, edging to the very hair-line of the magic circle, which seemed to assure their placid sunny peace. An upheaval of splintered granite often tossed and tumbled in the abandon of an unrestrained passion that seemed irresistibly to overwhelm the sanities of a whole region; but somewhere, in the very forefront of turmoil, was like to slumber one of these little meadows, as unconscious of anything but its own flawless green simplicity as a child asleep in mid-ocean. Or, away up in the snows, warmed by the fortuity of reflected heat, its emerald eye looked bravely out to the heavens. Or, as here, it rested confidingly in the very heart of the austere forest.

Always these parks are green; always are they clear and open. Their size varies widely. Some are as little as a city lawn; others, like the great Monache, [2] are miles in extent. In them resides the possibility of your traveling the high country; for they supply the feed for your horses.

[2] Do not fail to sound the final e.

Being desert-weary, the Tenderfoot and I cried out with the joy of it, and told in extravagant language how this was the best camp we had ever made.

"It's a bum camp," growled Wes. "If we couldn't get better camps than this, I'd quit the game."

He expatiated on the fact that this particular meadow was somewhat boggy; that the feed was too watery; that there'd be a cold wind down through the pines; and other small and minor details. But we, our backs propped against appropriately slanted rocks, our pipes well aglow, gazed down the twilight through the wonderful great columns of the trees to where the white horses shone like snow against the unaccustomed relief of green, and laughed him to scorn. What did we - or the horses for that matter - care for trifling discomforts of the body? In these intangible comforts of the eye was a great refreshment of the spirit.

The following day we rode through the pine forests growing on the ridges and hills and in the elevated bowl-like hollows. These were not the so-called "big trees," - with those we had to do later, as you shall see. They were merely sugar and yellow pines, but never anywhere have I seen finer specimens. They were planted with a grand sumptuousness of space, and their trunks were from five to twelve feet in diameter and upwards of two hundred feet high to the topmost spear. Underbrush, ground growth, even saplings of the same species lacked entirely, so that we proceeded in the clear open aisles of a tremendous and spacious magnificence.

This very lack of the smaller and usual growths, the generous plan of spacing, and the size of the trees themselves necessarily deprived us of a standard of comparison. At first the forest seemed immense. But after a little our eyes became accustomed to its proportions. We referred it back to the measures of long experience. The trees, the wood-aisles, the extent of vision shrunk to the normal proportions of an Eastern pinery. And then we would lower our gaze.

Stewart Edward White

The pack-train would come into view. It had become lilliputian, the horses small as white mice, the men like tin soldiers, as though we had undergone an enchantment. But in a moment, with the rush of a mighty transformation, the great trees would tower huge again.

In the pine woods of the mountains grows also a certain close-clipped parasitic moss. In color it is a brilliant yellow-green, more yellow than green. In shape it is crinkly and curly and tangled up with itself like very fine shavings. In consistency it is dry and brittle. This moss girdles the trunks of trees with innumerable parallel inch-wide bands a foot or so apart, in the manner of old-fashioned striped stockings. It covers entirely sundry twigless branches. Always in appearance is it fantastic, decorative, almost Japanese, as though consciously laid in with its vivid yellow-green as an intentional note of a tone scheme. The somberest shadows, the most neutral twilights, the most austere recesses are lighted by it as though so many freakish sunbeams had severed relations with the parent luminary to rest quietly in the coolnesses of the ancient forest.

Underfoot the pine-needles were springy beneath the horse's hoof. The trail went softly, with the courtesy of great gentleness. Occasionally we caught sight of other ridges, - also with pines, - across deep sloping valleys, pine filled. The effect of the distant trees seen from above was that of roughened velvet, here smooth and shining, there dark with rich shadows. On these slopes played the wind. In the level countries it sang through the forest progressively: here on the slope it struck a thousand trees at once. The air was ennobled with the great voice, as a church is ennobled by the tones of a great organ. Then we would drop back again to the inner country, for our way did not contemplate the descents nor climbs, but held to the general level of a plateau.

Clear fresh brooks ran in every ravine. Their water was snow-white against the black rocks; or lay dark in bank-shadowed pools. As our horses splashed across we could glimpse the rainbow trout flashing to cover. Where the watered hollows grew lush were thickets full of birds, outposts of the aggressively and cheerfully worldly in this pine-land of spiritual detachment. Gorgeous bush-flowers, great of petal as magnolias, with perfume that lay on the air like a heavy drowsiness; long clear stretches of an ankle-high shrub of vivid emerald, looking in the distance like sloping meadows of a peculiar color-brilliance; patches of smaller flowers where for the trifling space of a street's width the sun had unobstructed fall, - these from time to time diversified the way, brought to our perceptions the endearing trifles of earthiness, of humanity, befittingly to modify the austerity of the great forest. At a brookside we saw, still fresh and moist, the print of a bear's foot. From a patch of the little emerald brush, a barren doe rose to her feet, eyed us a moment, and then bounded away as though propelled by springs. We saw her from time to time surmounting little elevations farther and farther away.

The air was like cold water. We had not lung capacity to satisfy our desire for it. There came with it a dry exhilaration that brought high spirits, an optimistic viewpoint, and a tremendous keen appetite. It seemed that we could never tire. In fact we never did. Sometimes, after a particularly hard day, we felt like resting; but it was always after the day's work was done, never while it was under way. The Tenderfoot and I one day went afoot twenty-two miles up and down a mountain fourteen thousand feet high. The last three thousand feet were nearly straight up and down. We finished at a four-mile clip an hour before sunset, and discussed what to do next to fill in the time. When we sat down, we found we had had about enough; but we had not discovered it before.

All of us, even the morose and cynical Dinkey, felt the benefit of the change from the lower country. Here we were definitely in the Mountains. Our plateau ran from six to eight thousand feet in altitude. Beyond it occasionally we could see three more ridges, rising and falling, each higher than the last. And then, in the blue distance, the very crest of the broad system called the Sierras, - another wide region of sheer granite rising in peaks, pinnacles, and minarets, rugged, wonderful, capped with the eternal snows.

IX

THE TRAIL

When you say "trail" to a Westerner, his eye lights up. This is because it means something to him. To another it may mean something entirely different, for the blessed word is of that rare and beautiful category which is at once of the widest significance and the most intimate privacy to him who utters it. To your mind leaps the picture of the dim forest-aisles and the murmurings of tree-top breezes; to him comes a vision of the wide dusty desert; to me, perhaps, a high wild country of wonder. To all of us it is the slender, unbroken, never-ending thread connecting experiences.

For in a mysterious way, not to be understood, our trails never do end. They stop sometimes, and wait patiently while we dive in and out of houses, but always when we are ready to go on, they are ready too, and so take up the journey placidly as though nothing had intervened. They begin, when? Sometime, away in the past, you may remember a single episode, vivid through the mists of extreme youth. Once a very little boy walked with his father under a green roof of leaves that seemed farther than the sky and as unbroken. All of a sudden the man raised his gun and fired upwards, apparently through the green roof. A pause ensued. Then, hurtling roughly through still that same green roof, a great bird fell, hitting the earth with a thump. The very little boy was I. My trail must have begun there under the bright green roof of leaves.

From that earliest moment the Trail unrolls behind you like a thread so that never do you quite lose connection with your selves. There is something a little fearful to the imaginative in the insistence of it. You may camp, you may linger, but some time or another, sooner or later, you must go on, and when you do, then once again the Trail takes up its continuity without reference to the muddied place you have tramped out in your indecision or indolence or obstinacy or necessity. It would be exceedingly curious to follow out in patience the chart of a man's going, tracing the pattern of his steps with all its windings of nursery, playground, boys afield, country, city, plain, forest, mountain, wilderness, home, always on and on into the higher country of responsibility until at the last it leaves us at the summit of the Great Divide. Such a pattern would tell his story as surely as do the tracks of a partridge on the snow.

A certain magic inheres in the very name, or at least so it seems to me. I should be interested to know whether others feel the same glamour that I do in the contemplation of such syllables as the Lo-Lo Trail, the Tunemah Trail, the Mono Trail, the Bright Angel Trail. A certain elasticity of application too leaves room for the more connotation. A trail may be almost anything. There are wagon-trails which East would rank as macadam roads; horse-trails that would compare favorably with our best bridle-paths; foot-trails in the fur country worn by constant use as smooth as so many garden-walks. Then again there are other arrangements. I have heard a mule-driver overwhelmed with skeptical derision because he claimed to have upset but six times in traversing a certain bit of trail not over five miles long; in charts of the mountains are marked many trails which are only "ways through," - you will find few traces of predecessors; the same can be said of trails in the great forests where even an Indian is sometimes at fault. "Johnny, you're lost," accused the white man. "Trail lost: Injun here," denied the red man. And so after your experience has led you by the campfires of a thousand delights, and each of those campfires is on the Trail, which only pauses courteously for your stay and then leads on untiring into new mysteries forever and ever, you come to love it as the donor of great joys. You too become a Westerner, and when somebody says "trail," your eye too lights up.

The general impression of any particular trail is born rather of the little incidents than of the big accidents. The latter are exotic, and might belong to any time or places; the former are individual. For the Trail is a vantage-ground, and from it, as your day's travel unrolls, you see many things. Nine tenths of your experience comes thus, for in the long journeys the side excursions are few enough and unimportant enough almost to merit classification with the accidents. In time the character of the Trail thus defines itself.

Most of all, naturally, the kind of country has to do with this generalized impression. Certain surprises, through trees, of vista looking out over unexpected spaces; little notches in the hills beyond which you gain to a placid far country sleeping under a sun warmer than your elevation permits; the delicious excitement of the moment when you approach the very knife-edge of the summit and wonder what lies beyond, - these are the things you remember with a warm heart. Your saddle is a point of vantage. By it you are elevated above the country; from it you can see clearly. Quail scuttle away to right and left, heads ducked low; grouse boom solemnly on the rigid limbs of pines; deer vanish through distant thickets to appear on yet more distant ridges, thence to gaze curiously, their great ears forward; across the canon the bushes sway violently with the passage of a cinnamon bear among them, - you see them all from your post of observation. Your senses are always alert for these things; you are always bending from your saddle to examine the tracks and signs that continually offer themselves for your inspection and interpretation.

Our trail of this summer led at a general high elevation, with comparatively little climbing and comparatively easy traveling for days at a time. Then suddenly we would find ourselves on the brink of a great box canon from three to seven thousand feet deep, several miles wide, and utterly precipitous. In the bottom of this canon would be good feed, fine groves of trees, and a river of some size in which swam fish. The trail to the canon-bed was always bad, and generally dangerous. In many instances we found it bordered with the bones of horses that had failed. The river had somehow to be forded. We would camp a day or so in the good feed and among the fine groves of trees, fish in the river, and then address ourselves with much reluctance to the ascent of the other bad and dangerous trail on the other side. After that, in the natural course of events, subject to variation, we could expect nice trails, the comfort of easy travel, pines, cedars, redwoods, and joy of life until another great cleft opened before us or another great mountain-pass barred our way.

This was the web and woof of our summer. But through it ran the patterns of fantastic delight such as the West alone can offer a man's utter disbelief in them. Some of these patterns stand out in memory with peculiar distinctness.

Below Farewell Gap is a wide canon with high walls of dark rock, and down those walls run many streams of water. They are white as snow with the dash of their descent, but so distant that the eye cannot distinguish their motion. In the half light of dawn, with the yellow of sunrise behind the mountains, they look like gauze streamers thrown out from the windows of morning to celebrate the solemn pageant of the passing of many hills.

Again, I know of a canon whose westerly wall is colored in the dull rich colors, the fantastic patterns of a Moorish tapestry. Umber, seal brown, red, terra-cotta, orange, Nile green, emerald, purple, cobalt blue, gray, lilac, and many other colors, all rich with the depth of satin, glow wonderful as the craftiest textures. Only here the fabric is five miles long and half a mile wide.

There is no use in telling of these things. They, and many others of their like, are marvels, and exist; but you cannot tell about them, for the simple reason that the average reader concludes at once you must be exaggerating, must be carried away by the swing of words. The cold sober truth is, you cannot exaggerate. They haven't made the words. Talk as extravagantly as you wish to one who will in the most childlike manner believe every syllable you utter. Then take him into the Big Country. He will probably say, "Why, you didn't tell me it was going to be anything like THIS!" We in

Stewart Edward White

the East have no standards of comparison either as regards size or as regards color - especially color. Some people once directed me to "The Gorge" on the New England coast. I couldn't find it. They led me to it, and rhapsodized over its magnificent terror. I could have ridden a horse into the ridiculous thing. As for color, no Easterner believes in it when such men as Lungren or Parrish transposit it faithfully, any more than a Westerner would believe in the autumn foliage of our own hardwoods, or an Englishman in the glories of our gaudiest sunsets. They are all true.

In the mountains, the high mountains above the seven or eight thousand foot level, grows an affair called the snow-plant. It is, when full grown, about two feet in height, and shaped like a loosely constructed pine-cone set up on end. Its entire substance is like wax, and the whole concern - stalk, broad curling leaves, and all - is a brilliant scarlet. Sometime you will ride through the twilight of deep pine woods growing on the slope of the mountain, a twilight intensified, rendered more sacred to your mood by the external brilliancy of a glimpse of vivid blue sky above dazzling snow mountains far away. Then, in this monotone of dark green frond and dull brown trunk and deep olive shadow, where, like the ordered library of one with quiet tastes, nothing breaks the harmony of unobtrusive tone, suddenly flames the vivid red of a snow-plant. You will never forget it.

Flowers in general seem to possess this concentrated brilliancy both of color and of perfume. You will ride into and out of strata of perfume as sharply defined as are the quartz strata on the ridges. They lie sluggish and cloying in the hollows, too heavy to rise on the wings of the air.

As for color, you will see all sorts of queer things. The ordered flower-science of your childhood has gone mad. You recognize some of your old friends, but strangely distorted and changed, - even the dear old "butter 'n eggs" has turned pink! Patches of purple, of red, of blue, of yellow, of orange are laid in the hollows or on the slopes like brilliant blankets out to dry in the sun. The fine grasses are spangled with them, so that in the cup of the great fierce countries the meadows seem like beautiful green ornaments enameled with jewels. The Mariposa Lily, on the other hand, is a poppy-shaped flower varying from white to purple, and with each petal decorated by an "eye" exactly like those on the great Cecropia or Polyphemus moths, so that their effect is that of a flock of gorgeous butterflies come to rest. They hover over the meadows poised. A movement would startle them to flight; only the proper movement somehow never comes.

The great redwoods, too, add to the colored-edition impression of the whole country. A redwood, as perhaps you know, is a tremendous big tree sometimes as big as twenty feet in diameter. It is exquisitely proportioned like a fluted column of noble height. Its bark is slightly furrowed longitudinally, and of a peculiar elastic appearance that lends it an almost perfect illusion of breathing animal life. The color is a rich umber red. Sometimes in the early morning or the late afternoon, when all the rest of the forest is cast in shadow, these massive trunks will glow as though incandescent. The Trail, wonderful always, here seems to pass through the outer portals of the great flaming regions where dwell the risings and fallings of days.

As you follow the Trail up, you will enter also the permanent dwelling-places of the seasons. With us each visits for the space of a few months, then steals away to give place to the next. Whither they go you have not known until you have traveled the high mountains. Summer lives in the valley; that you know. Then a little higher you are in the spring-time, even in August. Melting patches of snow linger under the heavy firs; the earth is soggy with half-absorbed snow-water, trickling with exotic little rills that do not belong; grasses of the year before float like drowned hair in pellucid pools with an air of permanence, except for the one fact; fresh green things are sprouting bravely; through bare branches trickles a shower of bursting buds, larger at the top, as though the Sower had in passing scattered them from above. Birds of extraordinary cheerfulness sing merrily to new and doubtful flowers. The air tastes cold, but the sun is warm. The great spring humming and promise is in the air. And a few thousand feet higher you wallow over the surface of drifts while a winter wind searches your bones. I used to think that Santa Claus dwelt at the North Pole. Now I am convinced that he has a workshop somewhere among the great mountains where dwell the Seasons, and that his reindeer paw for grazing in the alpine meadows below the highest peaks.

Here the birds migrate up and down instead of south and north. It must be a great saving of trouble to them, and undoubtedly those who have discovered it maintain toward the unenlightened the same delighted and fraternal secrecy with which you and I guard the knowledge of a good trout-stream. When you can migrate adequately in a single day, why spend a month at it?

Also do I remember certain spruce woods with

openings where the sun shone through. The shadows were very black, the sunlight very white. As I looked back I could see the pack-horses alternately suffer eclipse and illumination in a strange flickering manner good to behold. The dust of the trail eddied and billowed lazily in the sun, each mote flashing as though with life; then abruptly as it crossed the sharp line of shade it disappeared.

From these spruce woods, level as a floor, we came out on the rounded shoulder of a mountain to find ourselves nearly nine thousand feet above the sea. Below us was a deep canon to the middle of the earth. And spread in a semicircle about the curve of our mountain a most magnificent panoramic view. First there were the plains, represented by a brown haze of heat; then, very remote, the foot-hills, the brush-hills, the pine mountains, the upper timber, the tremendous granite peaks, and finally the barrier of the main crest with its glittering snow. From the plains to that crest was over seventy miles. I should not dare say how far we could see down the length of the range; nor even how distant was the other wall of the canon over which we rode. Certainly it was many miles; and to reach the latter point consumed three days.

It is useless to multiply instances. The principle is well enough established by these. Whatever impression of your trail you carry away will come from the little common occurrences of every day. That is true of all trails; and equally so, it seems to me, of our Trail of Life sketched at the beginning of this essay.

But the trail of the mountains means more than wonder; it means hard work. Unless you stick to the beaten path, where the freighters have lost so many mules that they have finally decided to fix things up a bit, you are due for lots of trouble. Bad places will come to be a nightmare with you and a topic of conversation with whomever you may meet. We once enjoyed the company of a prospector three days while he made up his mind to tackle a certain bit of trail we had just descended. Our accounts did not encourage him. Every morning he used to squint up at the cliff which rose some four thousand feet above us. "Boys," he said finally as he started, "I may drop in on you later in the morning." I am happy to say he did not.

The most discouraging to the tenderfoot, but in reality the safest of all bad trails, is the one that skirts a precipice. Your horse possesses a laudable desire to spare your inside leg unnecessary abrasion, so he walks on the extreme outer edge. If you watch the performance of the animal ahead, you will observe that every few moments his outer hind hoof slips off that edge, knocking little stones down into the abyss. Then you conclude that sundry slight jars you have been experiencing are from the same cause. Your peace of mind deserts you. You stare straight ahead, sit VERY light indeed, and perhaps turn the least bit sick. The horse, however, does not mind, nor will you, after a little. There is absolutely nothing to do but to sit steady and give your animal his head. In a fairly extended experience I never got off the edge but once. Then somebody shot a gun immediately ahead; my horse tried to turn around, slipped, and slid backwards until he overhung the chasm. Fortunately his hind feet caught a tiny bush. He gave a mighty heave, and regained the trail. Afterwards I took a look and found that there were no more bushes for a hundred feet either way.

Next in terror to the unaccustomed is an ascent by lacets up a very steep side hill. The effect is cumulative. Each turn brings you one stage higher, adds definitely one more unit to the test of your hardihood. This last has not terrified you; how about the next? or the next? or the one after that? There is not the slightest danger. You appreciate this point after you have met head-on some old-timer. After you have speculated frantically how you are to pass him, he solves the problem by calmly turning his horse off the edge and sliding to the next lacet below. Then you see that with a mountain horse it does not much matter whether you get off such a trail or not.

The real bad places are quite as likely to be on the level as on the slant. The tremendous granite slides, where the cliff has avalanched thousands of tons of loose jagged rock-fragments across the passage, are the worst. There your horse has to be a goat in balance. He must pick his way from the top of one fragment to the other, and if he slips into the interstices he probably breaks a leg. In some parts of the granite country are also smooth rock aprons where footing is especially difficult, and where often a slip on them means a toboggan chute off into space. I know of one spot where such an apron curves off the shoulder of the mountain. Your horse slides directly down it until his hoofs encounter a little crevice. Checking at this, he turns sharp to the left and so off to the good trail again. If he does not check at the little crevice, he slides on over the curve of the shoulder and lands too far down to bury.

Loose rocks in numbers on a very steep and narrow trail are always an abomination, and a numerous abomination at that. A horse slides, skates, slithers. It has always seemed to me that luck must count largely in such a place. When the animal treads on a loose round stone - as he does every step of the way - that stone is going to roll under him, and he is going to catch himself as the nature of that stone and the little gods of chance may will. Only furthermore I have noticed that the really good horse keeps his feet, and the poor one tumbles. A judgmatical rider can help a great deal by the delicacy of his riding and the skill with which he uses his reins. Or better still, get off and walk.

Another mean combination, especially on a slant, is six inches of snow over loose stones or small boulders. There you hope for divine favor and flounder ahead. There is one compensation; the snow is soft to fall on. Boggy areas you must be able to gauge the depth of at a glance. And there are places, beautiful to behold, where a horse clambers up the least bit of an ascent, hits his pack against a projection, and is hurled into outer space. You must recognize these, for he will be busy with his feet.

Some of the mountain rivers furnish pleasing afternoons of sport. They are deep and swift, and below the ford are rapids. If there is a fallen tree of any sort across them, - remember the length of California trees, and do not despise the rivers, - you would better unpack, carry your goods across yourself, and swim the pack-horses. If the current is very bad, you can splice riatas, hitch one end to the horse and the other to a tree on the farther side, and start the combination. The animal is bound to swing across somehow. Generally you can drive them over loose. In swimming a horse from the saddle, start him well upstream to allow for the current, and never, never, never attempt to guide him by the bit. The Tenderfoot tried that at Mono Creek and nearly drowned himself and Old Slob. You would better let him alone, as he probably knows more than you do. If you must guide him, do it by hitting the side of his head with the flat of your hand.

Sometimes it is better that you swim. You can perform that feat by clinging to his mane on the downstream side, but it will be easier both for you and him if you hang to his tail. Take my word for it, he will not kick you.

Once in a blue moon you may be able to cross the whole outfit on logs. Such a log bridge spanned Granite Creek near the North Fork of the San Joaquin at an elevation of about seven thousand feet. It was suspended a good twenty feet above the water, which boiled white in a most disconcerting manner through a gorge of rocks. If anything fell off that log it would be of no further value even to the curiosity seeker. We got over all the horses save Tunemah. He refused to consider it, nor did peaceful argument win. As he was more or less of a fool, we did not take this as a reflection on our judgment, but culled cedar clubs. We beat him until we were ashamed. Then we put a slip-noose about his neck. The Tenderfoot and I stood on the log and heaved while Wes stood on the shore and pushed. Suddenly it occurred to me that if Tunemah made up his silly mind to come, he would probably do it all at once, in which case the Tenderfoot and I would have about as much show for life as fossil formations. I didn't say anything about it to the Tenderfoot, but I hitched my six-shooter around to the front, resolved to find out how good I was at wing-shooting horses. But

Stewart Edward White

Tunemah declared he would die for his convictions. "All right," said we, "die then," with the embellishment of profanity. So we stripped him naked, and stoned him into the raging stream, where he had one chance in three of coming through alive. He might as well be dead as on the other side of that stream. He won through, however, and now I believe he'd tackle a tight rope.

Of such is the Trail, of such its wonders, its pleasures, its little comforts, its annoyances, its dangers. And when you are forced to draw your six-shooter to end mercifully the life of an animal that has served you faithfully, but that has fallen victim to the leg-breaking hazard of the way, then you know a little of its tragedy also. May you never know the greater tragedy when a man's life goes out, and you unable to help! May always your trail lead through fine trees, green grasses, fragrant flowers, and pleasant waters!

X

ON SEEING DEER

Once I happened to be sitting out a dance with a tactful young girl of tender disposition who thought she should adapt her conversation to the one with whom she happened to be talking. Therefore she asked questions concerning out-of-doors. She knew nothing whatever about it, but she gave a very good imitation of one interested. For some occult reason people never seem to expect me to own evening clothes, or to know how to dance, or to be able to talk about anything civilized; in fact, most of them appear disappointed that I do not pull off a war-jig in the middle of the drawing-room.

This young girl selected deer as her topic. She mentioned liquid eyes, beautiful form, slender ears; she said "cute," and "darlings," and "perfect dears." Then she shuddered prettily.

"And I don't see how you can ever BEAR to shoot them, Mr. White," she concluded.

"You quarter the onions and slice them very thin," said I dreamily. "Then you take a little bacon fat you had left over from the flap-jacks and put it in the frying-pan. The frying-pan should be very hot. While the onions are frying, you must keep turning them over with a fork. It's rather difficult to get them all browned without burning some. I should broil the meat. A broiler is handy, but two willows, peeled and charred a little so the willow taste won't penetrate the meat, will do. Have the steak fairly thick. Pepper and salt it thoroughly. Sear it well at first in order to keep the juices in; then cook rather slowly. When it is done, put it on a hot plate and pour the browned onions, bacon fat and all, over it."

"What ARE you talking about?" she interrupted.

"I'm telling you why I can bear to shoot deer," said I.

"But I don't see - " said she.

"Don't you?" said I. "Well; suppose you've been climbing a mountain late in the afternoon when the sun is on the other side of it. It is a mountain of big boulders, loose little stones, thorny bushes. The slightest misstep would send pebbles rattling, brush rustling; but you have gone all the way without making that misstep. This is quite a feat. It means that you've known all about every footstep you've taken. That would be business enough for most people, wouldn't it? But in addition you've managed to see EVERYTHING on that side of the mountain - especially patches of brown. You've seen lots of patches of brown, and you've examined each one of them. Besides that, you've heard lots of little rustlings, and you've identified each one of them. To do all these things well keys your nerves to a high tension, doesn't it? And then near the top you look up from your last noiseless step to see in the brush a very dim patch of brown. If you hadn't been looking so hard, you surely wouldn't have made it out. Perhaps, if you're not humble-minded, you may reflect that most people wouldn't have seen it at all. You whistle once sharply. The patch of brown defines itself. Your heart gives one big jump. You know that you have but the briefest moment, the tiniest fraction of time, to hold the white bead of your rifle motionless and to press the trigger. It has to be done VERY steadily, at that distance, - and you out of breath, with your nerves keyed high in the tension of such caution."

"NOW what are you talking about?" she broke in helplessly.

"Oh, didn't I mention it?" I asked, surprised. "I was telling you why I could bear to shoot deer."

"Yes, but - " she began.

"Of course not," I reassured her. "After all, it's very simple. The reason I can bear to kill deer is because, to kill deer, you must accomplish a skillful elimination of the obvious."

My young lady was evidently afraid of being considered stupid; and also convinced of her inability to understand what I was driving at. So she temporized in the manner of society.

"I see," she said, with an air of complete enlightenment.

Now of course she did not see. Nobody could see the force of that last remark without the grace of further explanation, and yet in the elimination of the obvious rests the whole secret of seeing deer in the woods.

In traveling the trail you will notice two things: that a tenderfoot will habitually contemplate the horn of his saddle or the trail a few yards ahead of his horse's nose, with occasionally a look about at the landscape; and the old-timer will be constantly searching the prospect with keen understanding eyes. Now in the occasional glances the tenderfoot takes, his perceptions have room for just so many impressions. When the number is filled out he sees nothing more. Naturally the obvious features of the landscape supply the basis for these impressions. He sees the configuration of the mountains, the nature of their covering, the course of their ravines, first of all. Then if he looks more closely, there catches his eye an odd-shaped rock, a burned black stub, a flowering bush, or some such matter. Anything less striking in its appeal to the attention actually has not room for its recognition. In other words, supposing that a man has the natural ability to receive x visual impressions, the tenderfoot fills out his full capacity with the striking features of his surroundings. To be able to see anything more obscure in form or color, he must naturally put aside from his attention some one or another of these obvious features. He can, for example, look for a particular kind of flower on a side hill only by refusing to see other kinds.

If this is plain, then, go one step further in the logic of that reasoning. Put yourself in the mental attitude of a man looking for deer. His eye sweeps rapidly over a side hill; so rapidly that you cannot understand how he can have gathered the main features of that hill, let alone concentrate and refine his attention to the seeing of an animal under a bush. As a matter of fact he pays no attention to the main features. He has trained his eye, not so much to see things, as to leave things out.

The odd-shaped rock, the charred stub, the bright flowering bush do not exist for him. His eye passes over them as unseeing as yours over the patch of brown or gray that represents his quarry. His attention stops on the unusual, just as does yours; only in his case the unusual is not the obvious. He has succeeded by long training in eliminating that. Therefore he sees deer where you do not. As soon as you can forget the naturally obvious and construct an artificially obvious, then you too will see deer.

These animals are strangely invisible to the untrained eye even when they are standing "in plain sight." You can look straight at them, and not see them at all. Then some old woodsman lets you sight over his finger exactly to the spot. At once the figure of the deer fairly leaps into vision. I know of no more perfect example of the instantaneous than this. You are filled with astonishment that you could for a moment have avoided seeing it. And yet next time you will in all probability repeat just this "puzzle picture" experience.

The Tenderfoot tried for six weeks before he caught sight of one. He wanted to very much. Time and again one or the other of us would hiss back, "See the deer! over there by the yellow bush!" but before he could bring the deliberation of his scrutiny to the point of identification, the deer would be gone. Once a fawn jumped fairly within ten feet of the pack-horses and went bounding away through the bushes, and that fawn he could not help seeing. We tried conscientiously enough to get him a shot; but the Tenderfoot was unable to move through the brush less majestically than a Pullman car, so we had ended by becoming apathetic on the subject.

Finally, while descending a very abrupt mountain-side I made out a buck lying down perhaps three hundred feet directly below us. The buck was not looking our way, so I had time to call the Tenderfoot. He came. With difficulty and by using my rifle-barrel as a pointer I managed to show him the animal. Immediately he began to pant as though at the finish of a mile race, and his rifle, when he leveled it, covered a good half acre of ground. This would never do.

"Hold on!" I interrupted sharply.

He lowered his weapon to stare at me wild-eyed.

"What is it?" he gasped.

"Stop a minute!" I commanded. "Now take three deep breaths."

He did so.

"Now shoot," I advised, "and aim at his knees."

The deer was now on his feet and facing us, so the Tenderfoot had the entire length of the animal to allow for lineal variation. He fired. The deer dropped. The Tenderfoot thrust his hat over one eye, rested hand on hip in a manner cocky to behold.

"Simply slaughter!" he proffered with lofty scorn.

We descended. The bullet had broken the deer's back - about six inches from the tail. The Tenderfoot had overshot by at least three feet.

You will see many deer thus from the trail, -

in fact, we kept up our meat supply from the saddle, as one might say, - but to enjoy the finer savor of seeing deer, you should start out definitely with that object in view. Thus you have opportunity for the display of a certain finer woodcraft. You must know where the objects of your search are likely to be found, and that depends on the time of year, the time of days their age, their sex, a hundred little things. When the bucks carry antlers in the velvet, they frequent the inaccessibilities of the highest rocky peaks, so their tender horns may not be torn in the brush, but nevertheless so that the advantage of a lofty viewpoint may compensate for the loss of cover. Later you will find them in the open slopes of a lower altitude, fully exposed to the sun, that there the heat may harden the antlers. Later still, the heads in fine condition and tough to withstand scratches, they plunge into the dense thickets. But in the mean time the fertile does have sought a lower country with patches of small brush interspersed with open passages. There they can feed with their fawns, completely concealed, but able, by merely raising the head, to survey the entire landscape for the threatening of danger. The barren does, on the other hand, you will find through the timber and brush, for they are careless of all responsibilities either to offspring or headgear. These are but a few of the considerations you will take into account, a very few of the many which lend the deer countries strange thrills of delight over new knowledge gained, over crafty expedients invented or well utilized, over the satisfactory matching of your reason, your instinct, your subtlety and skill against the reason, instinct, subtlety, and skill of one of the wariest of large wild animals.

Perversely enough the times when you did NOT see deer are more apt to remain vivid in your memory than the times when you did. I can still see distinctly sundry wide jump-marks where the animal I was tracking had evidently caught sight of me and lit out before I came up to him. Equally, sundry little thin disappearing clouds of dust; cracklings of brush, growing ever more distant; the tops of bushes waving to the steady passage of something remaining persistently conce-aled, - these are the chief ingredients often repeated which make up deer-stalking memory. When I think of seeing deer, these things automatically rise.

A few of the deer actually seen do, however, stand out clearly from the many. When I was a very small boy possessed of a 32-20 rifle and large ambitions, I followed the advantage my father's footsteps made me in the deep snow of an unused logging-road. His attention was focused on some very interesting fresh tracks. I, being a small boy, cared not at all for tracks, and so saw a big doe emerge from the bushes not ten yards away, lope leisurely across the road, and disappear, wagging earnestly her tail. When I had recovered my breath I vehemently demanded the sense of fooling with tracks when there were real live deer to be had. My father examined me.

"Well, why didn't you shoot her?" he inquired dryly.

I hadn't thought of that.

In the spring of 1900 I was at the head of the Piant River waiting for the log-drive to start. One morning, happening to walk over a slashing of many years before in which had grown a strong thicket of white popples, I jumped a band of nine deer. I shall never forget the bewildering impression made by the glancing, dodging, bouncing white of those nine snowy tails and rumps.

But most wonderful of all was a great buck, of I should be afraid to say how many points, that stood silhouetted on the extreme end of a ridge high above our camp. The time was just after twilight, and as we watched, the sky lightened behind him in prophecy of the moon.

Stewart Edward White

XI

ON TENDERFEET

The tenderfoot is a queer beast. He makes more trouble than ants at a picnic, more work than a trespassing goat; he never sees anything, knows where anything is, remembers accurately your instructions, follows them if remembered, or is able to handle without awkwardness his large and pathetic hands and feet; he is always lost, always falling off or into things, always in difficulties; his articles of necessity are constantly being burned up or washed away or mislaid; he looks at you beamingly through great innocent eyes in the most chuckle-headed of manners; he exasperates you to within an inch of explosion, - and yet you love him.

I am referring now to the real tenderfoot, the fellow who cannot learn, who is incapable ever of adjusting himself to the demands of the wild life. Sometimes a man is merely green, inexperienced. But give him a chance and he soon picks up the game. That is your greenhorn, not your tenderfoot. Down near Monache meadows we came across an individual leading an old pack-mare up the trail. The first thing, he asked us to tell him where he was. We did so. Then we noticed that he carried his gun muzzle-up in his hip-pocket, which seemed to be a nice way to shoot a hole in your hand, but a poor way to make your weapon accessible.

He unpacked near us, and promptly turned the mare into a bog-hole because it looked green. Then he stood around the rest of the evening and talked deprecating talk of a garrulous nature.

"Which way did you come?" asked Wes.

The stranger gave us a hazy account of misnamed canons, by which we gathered that he had come directly over the rough divide below us.

"But if you wanted to get to Monache, why didn't you go around to the eastward through that pass, there, and save yourself all the climb? It must have been pretty rough through there."

"Yes, perhaps so," he hesitated. "Still - I got lots of time - I can take all summer, if I want to - and I'd rather stick to a straight line - then you know where you ARE - if you get off the straight line, you're likely to get lost, you know."

We knew well enough what ailed him, of course. He was a tenderfoot, of the sort that always, to its dying day, unhobbles its horses before putting their halters on. Yet that man for thirty-two years had lived almost constantly in the wild countries. He had traveled more miles with a pack-train than we shall ever dream of traveling, and hardly could we mention a famous camp of the last quarter century that he had not blundered into. Moreover he proved by the indirections of his misinformation that he had really been there and was not making ghost stories in order to impress us. Yet if the Lord spares him thirty-two years more, at the end of that time he will probably still be carrying his gun upside down, turning his horse into a bog-hole, and blundering through the country by main strength and awkwardness. He was a beautiful type of the tenderfoot.

The redeeming point of the tenderfoot is his humbleness of spirit and his extreme good nature. He exasperates you with his fool performances to the point of dancing cursing wild crying rage, and then accepts your - well, reproofs - so meekly that you come off the boil as though some one had removed you from the fire, and you feel like a low-browed thug.

Suppose your particular tenderfoot to be named Algernon. Suppose him to have packed his horse loosely - they always do - so that the pack has slipped, the horse has bucked over three square miles of assorted mountains, and the rest of the train is scattered over identically that area. You have run your saddle-horse to a lather heading the outfit. You have sworn and dodged and scrambled and yelled, even fired your six-shooter, to turn them and bunch them. In the mean time Algernon has either sat his horse like a park policeman in his leisure hours, or has ambled directly into your path of pursuit on an average of five times a minute. Then the trouble dies from the landscape and the baby bewilderment from his eyes. You slip from your winded horse and address Algernon with elaborate courtesy.

"My dear fellow," you remark, "did you not see that the thing for you to do was to head them down by the bottom of that little gulch there? Don't you really think ANYBODY would have seen it? What in hades do you think I wanted to run my horse all through those boulders for? Do you think I want to get him lame 'way up here in the hills? I don't mind telling a man a thing once, but to tell it to him fifty-eight times and then have it do no good - Have you the faintest recollection of my instructing you to turn the bight OVER instead of UNDER when you throw that pack-hitch? If you'd remember that, we shouldn't have had all this trouble."

"You didn't tell me to head them by the little gulch," babbles Algernon.

This is just the utterly fool reply that upsets your artificial and elaborate courtesy. You probably foam at the mouth, and dance on your hat, and shriek wild imploring imprecations to the astonished hills. This is not because you have an unfortunate disposition, but because Algernon has been doing precisely the same thing for two months.

"Listen to him!" you howl. "Didn't tell him! Why you gangle-legged bug-eyed soft-handed pop-eared tender-foot, you! there are some things you never THINK of telling a man. I never told you to open your mouth to spit, either. If you had a hired man at five dollars a year who was so all-around hopelessly thick-headed and incompetent as you are, you'd fire him to-morrow morning."

Then Algernon looks truly sorry, and doesn't answer back as he ought to in order to give occasion for the relief of a really soul-satisfying scrap, and utters the soft answer humbly. So your wrath is turned and there remain only the dregs which taste like some of Algernon's cooking.

It is rather good fun to relieve the bitterness of the heart. Let me tell you a few more tales of the tenderfoot, premising always that I love him, and when at home seek him out to smoke pipes at his fireside, to yarn over the trail, to wonder how much rancor he cherishes against the maniacs who declaimed against him, and by way of compensation to build up in the mind of his sweetheart, his wife, or his mother a fearful and wonderful reputation for him as the Terror of the Trail. These tales are selected from many, mere samples of a varied experience. They occurred here, there, and everywhere, and at various times. Let no one try to lay them at the door of our Tenderfoot merely because such is his title in this narrative. We called him that by way of distinction.

Once upon a time some of us were engaged in climbing a mountain rising some five thousand feet above our starting-place. As we toiled along, one of the pack-horses became impatient and pushed ahead. We did not mind that, especially, as long as she stayed in sight, but in a little while the trail was closed in by brush and timber.

"Algernon," said we, "just push on and get ahead of that mare, will you?"

Algernon disappeared. We continued to climb. The trail was steep and rather bad. The labor was strenuous, and we checked off each thousand feet with thankfulness. As we saw nothing further of Algernon, we naturally concluded he had headed the mare and was continuing on the trail. Then through a little opening we saw him riding cheerfully along without a care to occupy his mind. Just for luck we hailed him.

"Hi there, Algernon! Did you find her?"

"Haven't seen her yet."

"Well, you'd better push on a little faster. She may leave the trail at the summit."

Then one of us, endowed by heaven with a keen intuitive instinct for tenderfeet, - no one could have a knowledge of them, they are too unexpected, - had an inspiration.

"I suppose there are tracks on the trail ahead of you?" he called.

We stared at each other, then at the trail. Only one horse had preceded us, - that of the tenderfoot. But of course Algernon was nevertheless due for his chuckle-headed reply.

"I haven't looked," said he.

That raised the storm conventional to such an occasion.

"What in the name of seventeen little dicky-birds did you think you were up to!" we howled. "Were you going to ride ahead until dark in the childlike faith that that mare might show up somewhere? Here's a nice state of affairs. The trail is all tracked up now with our horses, and heaven knows whether she's left tracks where she turned off. It may be rocky there."

We tied the animals savagely, and started back on foot. It would be criminal to ask our saddle-horses to repeat that climb. Algernon we ordered to stay with them.

"And don't stir from them no matter what happens, or you'll get lost," we commanded out of the wisdom of long experience.

We climbed down the four thousand odd feet, and then back again, leading the mare. She had turned off not forty rods from where Algernon had taken up her pursuit.

Your Algernon never does get down to little details like tracks - his scheme of life is much too magnificent. To be sure he would not know fresh tracks from old if he should see them; so it is probably quite as well. In the morning he goes out after the horses. The bunch he finds easily enough, but one is missing. What would you do about it? You would naturally walk in a circle around the bunch until you crossed the track of the truant leading away from it, wouldn't you? If you made a wide enough circle you would inevitably cross that track, wouldn't you? provided the horse started out with the bunch in the first place. Then you would follow the track, catch the horse, and bring him back. Is this Algernon's procedure? Not any. "Ha!" says he, "old Brownie is missing. I will hunt him up." Then he maunders off into the scenery, trusting to high heaven that he is going to blunder against Brownie as a prominent feature of the landscape. After a couple of hours you probably saddle up Brownie and go out to find the tenderfoot.

He has a horrifying facility in losing himself. Nothing is more cheering than to arise from a hard-earned couch of ease for the purpose of trailing an Algernon or so through the gathering dusk to the spot where he has managed to find something - a very real despair of ever getting back to food and warmth. Nothing is more irritating then than his gratitude.

I traveled once in the Black Hills with such a tenderfoot. We were off from the base of supplies for a ten days' trip with only a saddle-horse apiece. This was near first principles, as our total provisions consisted of two pounds of oatmeal, some tea, and sugar. Among other things we climbed Mt. Harney. The trail, after we left the horses, was as plain as a strip of Brussels carpet, but somehow or another that tenderfoot managed to get off it. I hunted him up. We gained the top, watched the sunset, and started down. The tenderfoot, I thought, was fairly at my coat-tails, but when I turned to speak to him he had gone; he must have turned off at one of the numerous little openings in the brush. I sat down to wait. By and by, away down the west slope of the mountain, I heard a shot, and a faint, a very faint, despairing yell. I, also, shot and yelled. After various signals of the sort, it became evident that the tenderfoot was approaching. In a moment he tore by at full speed, his hat off, his eye wild, his six-shooter popping at every jump. He passed within six feet of me, and never saw me. Subsequently I left him on the prairie, with accurate and simple instructions.

"There's the mountain range. You simply keep that to your left and ride eight hours. Then you'll see Rapid City. You simply CAN'T get lost. Those hills stick out like a sore thumb."

Two days later he drifted into Rapid City, having wandered off somewhere to the east. How he had done it I can never guess. That is his secret.

The tenderfoot is always in hard luck. Apparently, too, by all tests of analysis it is nothing but luck, pure chance, misfortune. And yet the very persistence of it in his case, where another escapes, perhaps indicates that much of what we call good luck is in reality unconscious skill in the arrangement of those elements which go to make up events. A persistently unlucky man is perhaps sometimes to be pitied, but more often to be booted. That philosophy will be cryingly unjust about once in ten.

But lucky or unlucky, the tenderfoot is human. Ordinarily that doesn't occur to you. He is a malevolent engine of destruction - quite as impersonal as heat or cold or lack of water. He is an unfortunate article of personal belonging requiring much looking after to keep in order. He is a credulous and convenient response to practical jokes, huge tales, misinformation. He is a laudable object of attrition for the development of your character. But somehow, in the woods, he is not as other men, and so you do not come to feel yourself in close human relations to him.

But Algernon is real, nevertheless. He has feelings, even if you do not respect them. He has his little enjoyments, even though he does rarely contemplate anything but the horn of his saddle.

"Algernon," you cry, "for heaven's sake stick that saddle of yours in a glass case and glut yourself with the sight of its ravishing beauties next WINTER. For the present do gaze on the mountains. That's what you came for."

No use.

He has, doubtless, a full range of all the appreciative emotions, though from his actions you'd never suspect it. Most human of all, he possesses his little vanities.

Algernon always overdoes the equipment question. If it is bird-shooting, he accumulates leggings and canvas caps and belts and dog-whistles and things until he looks like a picture from a department-store catalogue. In the cow country he wears Stetson hats, snake bands, red handkerchiefs, six-shooters, chaps, and huge spurs that do not match his face. If it is yachting, he has a chronometer with a gong in the cabin of a five-ton sailboat, possesses a nickle-plated machine to register the heel of his craft, sports a brass-bound yachting-cap and all the regalia. This is merely amusing. But I never could understand his insane desire to get sunburned. A man will get sunburned fast enough; he could not help it if he would. Algernon usually starts out from town without a hat. Then he dares not take off his sweater for a week lest it carry away his entire face. I have seen men with deep sores on their shoulders caused by nothing but excessive burning in the sun. This, too, is merely amusing. It means quite simply that Algernon realizes his inner deficiencies and wants to make up for them by the outward seeming. Be kind to him, for he has been raised a pet.

The tenderfoot is lovable - mysterious in how he does it - and awfully unexpected.

XII

THE CANON

One day we tied our horses to three bushes, and walked on foot two hundred yards. Then we looked down.

It was nearly four thousand feet down. Do you realize how far that is? There was a river meandering through olive-colored forests. It was so distant that it was light green and as narrow as a piece of tape. Here and there were rapids, but so remote that we could not distinguish the motion of them, only the color. The white resembled tiny dabs of cotton wool stuck on the tape. It turned and twisted, following the turns and twists of the canon. Somehow the level at the bottom resembled less forests and meadows than a heavy and sluggish fluid like molasses flowing between the canon walls. It emerged from the bend of a sheer cliff ten miles to eastward: it disappeared placidly around the bend of another sheer cliff an equal distance to the westward.

The time was afternoon. As we watched, the shadow of the canon wall darkened the valley. Whereupon we looked up.

Now the upper air, of which we were dwellers for the

moment, was peopled by giants and clear atmosphere and glittering sunlight, flashing like silver and steel and precious stones from the granite domes, peaks, minarets, and palisades of the High Sierras. Solid as they were in reality, in the crispness of this mountain air, under the tangible blue of this mountain sky, they seemed to poise light as so many balloons. Some of them rose sheer, with hardly a fissure; some had flung across their shoulders long trailing pine draperies, fine as fur; others matched mantles of the whitest white against the bluest blue of the sky. Towards the lower country were more pines rising in ridges, like the fur of an animal that has been alarmed.

We dangled our feet over the edge and talked about it. Wes pointed to the upper end where the sluggish lava-like flow of the canon-bed first came into view.

"That's where we'll camp," said he.

"When?" we asked.

"When we get there," he answered.

For this canon lies in the heart of the mountains. Those who would visit it have first to get into the country - a matter of over a week. Then they have their choice of three probabilities of destruction.

The first route comprehends two final days of travel at an altitude of about ten thousand feet, where the snow lies in midsummer; where there is no feed, no comfort, and the way is strewn with the bones of horses. This is known as the "Basin Trail." After taking it, you prefer the others - until you try them.

The finish of the second route is directly over the summit of a mountain. You climb two thousand feet and then drop down five. The ascent is heart-breaking but safe. The descent is hair-raising and unsafe: no profanity can do justice to it. Out of a pack-train of thirty mules, nine were lost in the course of that five thousand feet. Legend has it that once many years ago certain prospectors took in a Chinese cook. At first the Mongolian bewailed his fate loudly and fluently, but later settled to a single terrified moan that sounded like "tu-ne-mah! tu-ne-mah!" The trail was therefore named the "Tu-ne-mah Trail." It is said that "tu-ne-mah" is the very worst single vituperation of which the Chinese language is capable.

The third route is called "Hell's Half Mile." It is not misnamed.

Thus like paradise the canon is guarded; but like paradise it is wondrous in delight. For when you descend you find that the tape-wide trickle of water seen from above has become a river with profound darkling pools and placid stretches and swift dashing rapids; that the dark green sluggish flow in the canon-bed has disintegrated into a noble forest with great pine-trees, and shaded aisles, and deep dank thickets, and brush openings where the sun is warm and the birds are cheerful, and groves of cottonwoods where all day long softly, like snow, the flakes of cotton float down through the air. Moreover there are meadows, spacious lawns, opening out, closing in, winding here and there through the groves in the manner of spilled naphtha, actually waist high with green feed, sown with flowers like a brocade. Quaint tributary little brooks babble and murmur down through these trees, down through these lawns. A blessed warm sun hums with the joy of innumerable bees. To right hand and to left, in front of you and behind, rising sheer, forbidding, impregnable, the cliffs, mountains, and ranges hem you in. Down the river ten miles you can go: then the gorge closes, the river grows savage, you can only look down the tumbling fierce waters and turn back. Up the river five miles you can go, then interpose the sheer snow-clad cliffs of the Palisades, and them, rising a matter of fourteen thousand feet, you may not cross. You are shut in your paradise as completely as though surrounded by iron bars.

But, too, the world is shut out. The paradise is yours. In it are trout and deer and grouse and bear and lazy happy days. Your horses feed to the fatness of butter. You wander at will in the ample though definite limits of your domain. You lie on your back and examine dispassionately, with an interest entirely detached, the huge cliff-walls of the valley. Days slip by. Really, it needs at least an angel with a flaming sword to force you to move on.

We turned away from our view and addressed ourselves to the task of finding out just when we were going to get there. The first day we bobbed up and over innumerable little ridges of a few hundred feet elevation, crossed several streams, and skirted the wide bowl-like amphitheatre of a basin. The second day we climbed over things and finally ended in a small hanging park named Alpine Meadows, at an elevation of eight thousand five hundred feet. There we rested-over a day, camped under a single pine-tree, with the quick-growing mountain grasses thick about us, a semicircle of mountains on three sides, and the plunge into the canon on the other. As we needed meat, we spent part of the day in finding a deer. The rest of the time we watched idly for bear.

Bears are great travelers. They will often go twenty miles overnight, apparently for the sheer delight of being on the move. Also are they exceedingly loath to expend unnecessary energy in getting to places, and they hate to go down steep hills. You see, their fore legs are short. Therefore they are skilled in the choice of easy routes through the mountains, and once having made the choice they stick to it until through certain narrow places on the route selected they have worn a trail as smooth as a garden-path. The old prospectors used quite occasionally to pick out the horse-passes by trusting in general to the bear migrations, and many a well-traveled route of to-day is superimposed over the way-through picked out by old bruin long ago.

Of such was our own trail. Therefore we kept our rifles at hand and our eyes open for a straggler. But none came, though we baited craftily with portions of our deer. All we gained was a rattlesnake, and he seemed a bit out of place so high up in the air.

Mount Tunemah stood over against us, still twenty-two hundred feet above our elevation. We gazed on it sadly, for directly by its summit, and for five hours beyond, lay our trail, and evil of reputation was that trail beyond all others. The horses, as we bunched them in preparation for the packing, took on a new interest, for it was on the cards that the unpacking at evening would find some missing from the ranks.

"Lily's a goner, sure," said Wes. "I don't know how she's got this far except by drunken man's luck. She'll never make the Tunemah."

"And Tunemah himself," pointed out the Tenderfoot, naming his own fool horse; "I see where I start in to walk."

"Sort of a `morituri te salutamur,' " said I.

We climbed the two thousand two hundred feet, leading our saddle-horses to save their strength. Every twenty feet we rested, breathing heavily of the rarified air. Then at the top of the world we paused on the brink of nothing to tighten cinches, while the cold wind swept by us, the snow glittered in a sunlight become silvery like that of early April, and the giant peaks of the High Sierras lifted into a distance inconceivably remote, as though the horizon had been set back for their accommodation.

To our left lay a windrow of snow such as you will see drifted into a sharp crest across a corner of your yard; only this windrow was twenty feet high and packed solid by the sun, the wind, and the weight of its age. We climbed it and looked over directly into the eye of a round Alpine lake seven or eight hundred feet below. It was of an intense cobalt blue, a color to be seen only in these glacial bodies of water, deep and rich as the mantle of a merchant of Tyre. White ice floated in it. The savage fierce granite needles and knife-edges of the mountain crest hemmed it about.

But this was temporizing, and we knew it. The first drop of the trail was so steep that we could flip a pebble to the first level of it, and so rough in its water-and-snow-gouged knuckles of rocks that it seemed that at the first step a horse must necessarily fall end over end. We made it successfully, however, and breathed deep. Even Lily, by a miracle of lucky scrambling, did not even stumble.

"Now she's easy for a little ways," said Wes, "then we'll get busy."

When we "got busy" we took our guns in our hands to preserve them from a fall, and started in. Two more miracles saved Dinkey at two more places. We spent an hour at one spot, and finally built a new trail around it. Six times a minute we held our breaths and stood on tiptoe with anxiety, powerless to help, while the horse did his best. At the especially bad places we checked them off one after another, congratulating ourselves on so much saved as each came across without accident. When there were no bad places, the trail was so extraordinarily steep that we ahead were in constant dread of a horse's falling on us from behind, and our legs did become wearied to incipient paralysis by the constant stiff checking of the descent. Moreover every second or so one of the big loose stones with which the trail was cumbered would be dislodged and come bouncing down among us. We dodged and swore; the horses kicked; we all feared for the integrity of our legs. The day was full of an intense nervous strain, an entire absorption in the precise present. We promptly forgot a difficulty as soon as we were by it: we had not time to think of those still ahead. All outside the insistence of the moment was blurred and unimportant, like a specialized focus, so I cannot tell you much about the scenery. The only outside impression we received was that the canon floor was slowly rising to meet us.

Then strangely enough, as it seemed, we stepped off to level ground.

Our watches said half-past three. We had made five miles in a little under seven hours.

Remained only the crossing of the river. This was no mean task, but we accomplished it lightly, searching out a ford. There were high grasses, and on the other side of them a grove of very tall cottonwoods, clean as a park. First of all we cooked things; then we spread things; then we lay on our backs and smoked things, our hands clasped back of our heads. We cocked ironical eyes at the sheer cliff of old Mount Tunemah, very much as a man would cock his eye at a tiger in a cage.

Already the meat-hawks, the fluffy Canada jays, had found us out, and were prepared to swoop down boldly on whatever offered to their predatory skill. We had nothing for them yet, - there were no remains of the lunch, - but the fire-irons were out, and ribs of venison were roasting slowly over the coals in preparation for the evening meal. Directly opposite, visible through the lattice of the trees, were two huge mountain peaks, part of the wall that shut us in, over against us in a height we had not dared ascribe to the sky itself. By and by the shadow of these mountains rose on the westerly wall. It crept up at first slowly, extinguishing color; afterwards more rapidly as the sun approached the horizon. The sunlight disappeared. A moment's gray intervened, and then the wonderful golden afterglow laid on the peaks its enchantment. Little by little that too faded, until at last, far away, through a rift in the ranks of the giants, but one remained gilded by the glory of a dream that continued with it after the others. Heretofore it had seemed to us an insignificant peak, apparently overtopped by many, but by this token we knew it to be the highest of them all.

Stewart Edward White

Then ensued another pause, as though to give the invisible scene-shifter time to accomplish his work, followed by a shower of evening coolness, that seemed to sift through the trees like a soft and gentle rain. We ate again by the flicker of the fire, dabbing a trifle uncertainly at the food, wondering at the distant mountain on which the Day had made its final stand, shrinking a little before the stealthy dark that flowed down the canon in the manner of a heavy smoke.

In the notch between the two huge mountains blazed a star, - accurately in the notch, like the front sight of a rifle sighted into the marvelous depths of space. Then the moon rose.

First we knew of it when it touched the crest of our two mountains. The night has strange effects on the hills. A moment before they had menaced black and sullen against the sky, but at the touch of the moon their very substance seemed to dissolve, leaving in the upper atmosphere the airiest, most nebulous, fragile, ghostly simulacrums of themselves you could imagine in the realms of fairy-land. They seemed actually to float, to poise like cloud-shapes about to dissolve. And against them were cast the inky silhouettes of three fir-trees in the shadow near at hand.

Down over the stones rolled the river, crying out to us with the voices of old accustomed friends in another wilderness. The winds rustled.

XIII

TROUT, BUCKSKIN, AND PROSPECTORS

As I have said, a river flows through the canon. It is a very good river with some riffles that can be waded down to the edges of black pools or white chutes of water; with appropriate big trees fallen slantwise into it to form deep holes; and with hurrying smooth stretches of some breadth. In all of these various places are rainbow trout.

There is no use fishing until late afternoon. The clear sun of the high altitudes searches out mercilessly the bottom of the stream, throwing its miniature boulders, mountains, and valleys as plainly into relief as the buttes of Arizona at noon. Then the trout quite refuse. Here and there, if you walk far enough and climb hard enough over all sorts of obstructions, you may discover a few spots shaded by big trees or rocks where you can pick up a half dozen fish; but it is slow work. When, however, the shadow of the two huge mountains feels its way across the stream, then, as though a signal had been given, the trout begin to rise. For an hour and a half there is noble sport indeed.

The stream fairly swarmed with them, but of course some places were better than others. Near the upper reaches the water boiled like seltzer around the base of a tremendous tree. There the pool was at least ten feet deep and shot with bubbles throughout the whole of its depth, but it was full of fish. They rose eagerly to your gyrating fly, - and took it away with them down to subaqueous chambers and passages among the roots of that tree. After which you broke your leader. Royal Coachman was the best lure, and therefore valuable exceedingly were Royal Coachmen. Whenever we lost one we lifted up our voices in lament, and went away from there, calling to mind that there were other pools, many other pools, free of obstruction and with fish in them. Yet such is the perversity of fishermen, we were back losing more Royal Coachmen the very next day. In all I managed to disengage just three rather small trout from that pool, and in return decorated their ancestral halls with festoons of leaders and the brilliance of many flies.

Now this was foolishness. All you had to do was to walk through a grove of cottonwoods, over a brook, through another grove of pines, down a sloping meadow to where one of the gigantic pine-trees had obligingly spanned the current. You crossed that, traversed another meadow, broke through a thicket, slid down a steep grassy bank, and there you were. A great many years before a pine-tree had fallen across the current. Now its whitened skeleton lay there, opposing a barrier for about twenty-five feet out into the stream. Most of the water turned aside, of course, and boiled frantically around the end as though trying to catch up with the rest of the stream which had gone on without it, but some of it dived down under and came up on the other side. There, as though bewildered, it paused in an uneasy pool. Its constant action had excavated a very deep hole, the debris of which had formed a bar immediately below. You waded out on the bar and cast along the length of the pine skeleton over the pool.

If you were methodical, you first shortened your line, and began near the bank, gradually working out until you were casting forty-five feet to the very edge of the fast current. I know of nothing pleasanter for you to do. You see, the evening shadow was across the river, and a beautiful grass slope at your back. Over the way was a grove of trees whose birds were very busy because it was near their sunset, while towering over them were mountains, quite peaceful by way of contrast because THEIR sunset was still far distant. The river was in a great hurry, and was talking to itself like a man who has been detained and is now at last making up time to his important engagement. And from the deep black shadow beneath the pine skeleton, occasionally flashed white bodies that made concentric circles where they broke the surface of the water, and which fought you to a finish in the glory of battle. The casting was against the current, so your flies could rest but the briefest possible moment on the surface of the stream. That moment was enough. Day after day you could catch your required number from an apparently inexhaustible supply.

I might inform you further of the gorge downstream, where you lie flat on your stomach ten feet above the river, and with one hand cautiously extended over the edge cast accurately into the angle of the cliff. Then when you get your strike, you tow him downstream, clamber precariously to the water's level - still playing your fish - and there land him, - if he has accommodatingly stayed hooked. A three-pound fish will make you a lot of tribulation at this game.

We lived on fish and venison, and had all we wanted. The bear-trails were plenty enough, and the signs were comparatively fresh, but at the time of our visit the animals themselves had gone over the mountains on some sort of a picnic. Grouse, too, were numerous in the popple thickets, and flushed much like our ruffed grouse of the East. They afforded first-rate wing-shooting for Sure-Pop, the little shot-gun.

But these things occupied, after all, only a small part of every day. We had loads of time left. Of course we explored the valley up and down. That occupied two days. After that we became lazy. One always does in a permanent camp. So did the horses. Active - or rather restless interest in life seemed to die away. Neither we nor they had to rustle hard for food. They became fastidious in their choice, and at all times of day could be seen sauntering in Indian file from one part of the meadow to the other for the sole purpose apparently of cropping a half dozen indifferent mouthfuls. The rest of the time they roosted under trees, one hind leg relaxed, their eyes half closed, their ears wabbling, the pictures of imbecile content. We were very much the same.

Of course we had our outbursts of virtue. While under their influence we undertook vast works. But after their influence had died out, we found ourselves with said vast works on our hands, and so came to cursing ourselves and our fool spasms of industry.

For instance, Wes and I decided to make buckskin from the hide of the latest deer. We did not need the buckskin - we already had two in the pack. Our ordinary procedure would have been to dry the hide for future treatment by a Mexican, at a dollar a hide, when we should have returned home. But, as I said, we were afflicted by sporadic activity, and wanted to do something.

We began with great ingenuity by constructing a graining-tool out of a table-knife. We bound it with rawhide, and encased it with wood, and wrapped it with cloth, and filed its edge square across, as is proper. After this we hunted out a very smooth, barkless log, laid the hide across it, straddled it, and began graining.

Graining is a delightful process. You grasp the tool by either end, hold the square edge at a certain angle, and push away from you mightily. A half-dozen pushes will remove a little patch of hair; twice as many more will scrape away half as much of the seal-brown grain, exposing the white of the hide. Then, if you want to, you can stop and establish in your mind a definite proportion between the amount thus exposed, the area remaining unexposed, and the muscular fatigue of these dozen and a half of mighty pushes. The proportion will be wrong. You have left out of account the fact that you are going to get almighty sick of the job; that your arms and upper back are going to ache shrewdly before you are done; and that as you go on it is going to be increasingly difficult to hold down the edges firmly enough to offer the required resistance to your knife. Besides - if you get careless - you'll scrape too hard: hence little holes in the completed buckskin. Also - if you get careless - you will probably leave the finest, tiniest shreds of grain, and each of them means a hard transparent spot in the product. Furthermore, once having started in on the job, you are like the little boy who caught the trolley: you cannot let go. It must be finished immediately, all at one heat, before the hide stiffens.

Be it understood, your first enthusiasm has evaporated, and you are thinking of fifty pleasant things you might just as well be doing.

Next you revel in grease, - lard oil, if you have it; if not, then lard, or the product of boiled brains. This you must rub into the skin. You rub it in until you suspect that your finger-nails have worn away, and you glisten to the elbows like an Eskimo cutting blubber.

By the merciful arrangement of those who invented buckskin, this entitles you to a rest. You take it - for several days - until your conscience seizes you by the scruff of the neck.

Then you transport gingerly that slippery, clammy, soggy, snaky, cold bundle of greasy horror to the bank of the creek, and there for endless hours you wash it. The grease is more reluctant to enter the stream than you are in the early morning. Your hands turn purple. The others go by on their way to the trout-pools, but you are chained to the stake.

By and by you straighten your back with creaks, and walk home like a stiff old man, carrying your hide rid of all superfluous oil. Then if you are just learning how, your instructor examines the result.

"That's all right," says he cheerfully. "Now when it dries, it will be buckskin."

That encourages you. It need not. For during the process of drying it must be your pastime constantly to pull and stretch at every square inch of that boundless skin in order to loosen all the fibres. Otherwise it would dry as stiff as whalebone. Now there is nothing on earth that seems to dry slower than buckskin. You wear your fingers down to the first joints, and, wishing to preserve the remainder for future use, you carry the hide to your instructor.

"Just beginning to dry nicely," says he.

You go back and do it some more, putting the entire strength of your body, soul, and religious convictions into the stretching of that buckskin. It looks as white as paper; and feels as soft and warm as the turf on a southern slope. Nevertheless your tyrant declares it will not do.

"It looks dry, and it feels dry," says he, "but it isn't dry. Go to it!"

But at this point your outraged soul arches its back and bucks. You sneak off and roll up that piece of buckskin, and thrust it into the alforja. You KNOW it is dry. Then with a deep sigh of relief you come out of prison into the clear, sane, lazy atmosphere of the camp.

"Do you mean to tell me that there is any one chump enough to do that for a dollar a hide?" you inquire.

"Sure," say they.

"Well, the Fool Killer is certainly behind on his dates," you conclude.

About a week later one of your companions drags out of the alforja something crumpled that resembles in

Stewart Edward White

general appearance and texture a rusted five-gallon coal-oil can that has been in a wreck. It is only imperceptibly less stiff and angular and cast-iron than rawhide.

"What is this?" the discoverer inquires.

Then quietly you go out and sit on a high place before recognition brings inevitable - and sickening - chaff. For you know it at a glance. It is your buckskin.

Along about the middle of that century an old prospector with four burros descended the Basin Trail and went into camp just below us. Towards evening he sauntered in.

I sincerely wish I could sketch this man for you just as he came down through the fire-lit trees. He was about six feet tall, very leanly built, with a weather-beaten face of mahogany on which was superimposed a sweeping mustache and beetling eye-brows. These had originally been brown, but the sun had bleached them almost white in remarkable contrast to his complexion. Eyes keen as sunlight twinkled far down beneath the shadows of the brows and a floppy old sombrero hat. The usual flannel shirt, waistcoat, mountain-boots, and six-shooter completed the outfit. He might have been forty, but was probably nearer sixty years of age.

"Howdy, boys," said he, and dropped to the fireside, where he promptly annexed a coal for his pipe.

We all greeted him, but gradually the talk fell to him and Wes. It was commonplace talk enough from one point of view: taken in essence it was merely like the inquiry and answer of the civilized man as to another's itinerary - "Did you visit Florence? Berlin? St. Petersburg?" - and then the comparing of impressions. Only here again that old familiar magic of unfamiliar names threw its glamour over the terse sentences.

"Over beyond the Piute Monument," the old prospector explained, "down through the Inyo Range, a leetle north of Death Valley - "

"Back in seventy-eight when I was up in Bay Horse Canon over by Lost River - "

"Was you ever over in th' Panamit Mountains? - North of th' Telescope Range?" -

That was all there was to it, with long pauses for drawing at the pipes. Yet somehow in the aggregate that catalogue of names gradually established in the minds of us two who listened an impression of long years, of wide wilderness, of wandering far over the face of the earth. The old man had wintered here, summered a thousand miles away, made his strike at one end of the world, lost it somehow, and cheerfully tried for a repetition of his luck at the other. I do not believe the possibility of wealth, though always of course in the background, was ever near enough his hope to be considered a motive for action. Rather was it a dream, remote, something to be gained to-morrow, but never to-day, like the mediaeval Christian's idea of heaven. His interest was in the search. For that one could see in him a real enthusiasm. He had his smattering of theory, his very real empirical knowledge, and his superstitions, like all prospectors. So long as he could keep in grub, own a little train of burros, and lead the life he loved, he was happy.

Perhaps one of the chief elements of this remarkable interest in the game rather than the prizes of it was his desire to vindicate his guesses or his conclusions. He liked to predict to himself the outcome of his solitary operations, and then to prove that prediction through laborious days. His life was a gigantic game of solitaire. In fact, he mentioned a dozen of his claims many years apart which he had developed to a certain point, - "so I could see what they was," - and then abandoned in favor of fresher discoveries. He cherished the illusion that these were properties to whose completion some day he would return. But we knew better; he had carried them to the point where the result was no longer in doubt and then, like one who has no interest in playing on in an evidently prescribed order, had laid his cards on the table to begin a new game.

This man was skilled in his profession; he had pursued it for thirty odd years; he was frugal and industrious; undoubtedly of his long series of discoveries a fair percentage were valuable and are producing-properties to-day. Yet he confessed his bank balance to be less than five hundred dollars. Why was this? Simply and solely because he did not care. At heart it was entirely immaterial to him whether he ever owned a dollar above his expenses. When he sold his claims, he let them go easily, loath to bother himself with business details, eager to get away from the fuss and nuisance. The few hundred dollars he received he probably sunk in unproductive mining work, or was fleeced out of in the towns. Then joyfully he turned back to his beloved mountains and the life of his slow deep delight and his pecking away before the open doors of fortune. By and by he would build himself a little cabin down in the lower pine mountains, where he would grow a white beard, putter with occult wilderness crafts, and smoke long contemplative hours in the sun before his door. For tourists he would braid rawhide reins and quirts, or make buckskin. The jays and woodpeckers and Douglas squirrels would become fond of him. So he would be gathered to his fathers, a gentle old man whose life had been spent harmlessly in the open. He had had his ideal to which blindly he reached; he had in his indirect way contributed the fruits of his labor to mankind; his recompenses he had chosen according to his desires. When you consider these things, you perforce have to revise your first notion of him as a useless sort of old ruffian. As you come to know him better, you must love him for the kindliness, the simple honesty, the modesty, and charity that he seems to draw from his mountain environment. There are hundreds of him buried in the great canons of the West.

Our prospector was a little uncertain as to his plans. Along toward autumn he intended to land at some reputed placers near Dinkey Creek. There might be something in that district. He thought he would take a look. In the mean time he was just poking up through the country - he and his jackasses. Good way to spend the summer. Perhaps he might run across something 'most anywhere; up near the top of that mountain opposite looked mineralized. Didn't know but what he'd take a look at her to-morrow.

He camped near us during three days. I never saw a more modest, self-effacing man. He seemed genuinely, childishly, almost helplessly interested in our fly-fishing, shooting, our bear-skins, and our travels. You would have thought from his demeanor - which was sincere and not in the least ironical - that he had never seen or heard anything quite like that before, and was struck with wonder at it. Yet he had cast flies before we were born, and shot even earlier than he had cast a fly, and was a very Ishmael for travel. Rarely could you get an account of his own experiences, and then only in illustration of something else.

"If you-all likes bear-hunting," said he, "you ought to get up in eastern Oregon. I summered there once. The only trouble is, the brush is thick as hair. You 'most always have to bait them, or wait for them to come and drink. The brush is so small you ain't got much chance. I run onto a she-bear and cubs that way once. Didn't have nothin' but my six-shooter, and I met her within six foot."

He stopped with an air of finality.

"Well, what did you do?" we asked.

"Me?" he inquired, surprised. "Oh, I just leaked out of th' landscape."

He prospected the mountain opposite, loafed with us a little, and then decided that he must be going. About eight o'clock in the morning he passed us, hazing his burros, his tall, lean figure elastic in defiance of years.

"So long, boys," he called; "good luck!"

"So long," we responded heartily. "Be good to yourself."

He plunged into the river without hesitation, emerged dripping on the other side, and disappeared in the brush. From time to time during the rest of the morning we heard the intermittent tinkling of his bell-animal rising higher and higher above us on the trail.

In the person of this man we gained our first connection, so to speak, with the Golden Trout. He had caught some of them, and could tell us of their habits.

Few fishermen west of the Rockies have not heard of the Golden Trout, though, equally, few have much definite information concerning it. Such information usually runs about as follows:

It is a medium size fish of the true trout family, resembling a rainbow except that it is of a rich golden color. The peculiarity that makes its capture a dream to be dreamed of is that it swims in but one little stream of all the round globe. If you would catch a Golden Trout, you must climb up under the very base of the end of the High Sierras. There is born a stream that flows down from an elevation of about ten thousand feet to about eight thousand before it takes a long plunge into a branch of the Kern River. Over the twenty miles of its course you can cast your fly for Golden Trout; but what is the nature of that stream, that fish, or the method of its capture, few can tell you with any pretense of accuracy.

To be sure, there are legends. One, particularly striking, claims that the Golden Trout occurs in one other stream - situated in Central Asia! - and that the fish is therefore a remnant of some pre-glacial period, like Sequoia trees, a sort of grand-daddy of all trout, as it were. This is but a sample of what you will hear discussed.

Of course from the very start we had had our eye on

the Golden Trout, and intended sooner or later to work our way to his habitat. Our prospector had just come from there.

"It's about four weeks south, the way you and me travels," said he. "You don't want to try Harrison's Pass; it's chock full of tribulation. Go around by way of the Giant Forest. She's pretty good there, too, some sizable timber. Then over by Redwood Meadows, and Timber Gap, by Mineral King, and over through Farewell Gap. You turn east there, on a new trail. She's steeper than straight-up-an'-down, but shorter than the other. When you get down in the canon of Kern River, - say, she's a fine canon, too, - you want to go downstream about two mile to where there's a sort of natural over-flowed lake full of stubs stickin' up. You'll get some awful big rainbows in there. Then your best way is to go right up Whitney Creek Trail to a big high meadows mighty nigh to timber-line. That's where I camped. They's lots of them little yaller fish there. Oh, they bite well enough. You'll catch 'em. They's a little shy."

So in that guise - as the desire for new and distant things - did our angel with the flaming sword finally come to us.

We caught reluctant horses reluctantly. All the first day was to be a climb. We knew it; and I suspect that they knew it too. Then we packed and addressed ourselves to the task offered us by the Basin Trail.

XIV

ON CAMP COOKERY

One morning I awoke a little before the others, and lay on my back staring up through the trees. It was not my day to cook. We were camped at the time only about sixty-five hundred feet high, and the weather was warm. Every sort of green thing grew very lush all about us, but our own little space was held dry and clear for us by the needles of two enormous red cedars some four feet in diameter. A variety of thoughts sifted through my mind as it followed lazily the shimmering filaments of loose spider-web streaming through space. The last thought stuck. It was that that day was a holiday. Therefore I un-limbered my six-shooter, and turned her loose, each shot being accompanied by a meritorious yell.

The outfit boiled out of its blankets. I explained the situation, and after they had had some breakfast they agreed with me that a celebration was in order. Unanimously we decided to make it gastronomic.

"We will ride till we get to good feed," we concluded, "and then we'll cook all the afternoon. And nobody must eat anything until the whole business is prepared and served."

Stewart Edward White

It was agreed. We rode until we were very hungry, which was eleven o'clock. Then we rode some more. By and by we came to a log cabin in a wide fair lawn below a high mountain with a ducal coronet on its top, and around that cabin was a fence, and inside the fence a man chopping wood. Him we hailed. He came to the fence and grinned at us from the elevation of high-heeled boots. By this token we knew him for a cow-puncher.

"How are you?" said we.

"Howdy, boys," he roared. Roared is the accurate expression. He was not a large man, and his hair was sandy, and his eye mild blue. But undoubtedly his kinsmen were dumb and he had as birthright the voice for the entire family. It had been subsequently developed in the shouting after the wild cattle of the hills. Now his ordinary conversational tone was that of the announcer at a circus. But his heart was good.

"Can we camp here?" we inquired.

"Sure thing," he bellowed. "Turn your horses into the meadow. Camp right here."

But with the vision of a rounded wooded knoll a few hundred yards distant we said we'd just get out of his way a little. We crossed a creek, mounted an easy slope to the top of the knoll, and were delighted to observe just below its summit the peculiar fresh green hump which indicates a spring. The Tenderfoot, however, knew nothing of springs, for shortly he trudged a weary way back to the creek, and so returned bearing kettles of water. This performance hugely astonished the cowboy, who subsequently wanted to know if a "critter had died in the spring."

Wes departed to borrow a big Dutch oven of the man and to invite him to come across when we raised the long yell. Then we began operations.

Now camp cooks are of two sorts. Anybody can with a little practice fry bacon, steak, or flapjacks, and boil coffee. The reduction of the raw material to its most obvious cooked result is within the reach of all but the most hopeless tenderfoot who never knows the salt-sack from the sugar-sack. But your true artist at the business is he who can from six ingredients, by permutation, combination, and the genius that is in him turn out a full score of dishes. For simple example: GIVEN, rice, oatmeal, and raisins. Your expert accomplishes the following:

ITEM - Boiled rice.

ITEM - Boiled oatmeal.

ITEM - Rice boiled until soft, then stiffened by the addition of quarter as much oatmeal.

ITEM - Oatmeal in which is boiled almost to the dissolving point a third as much rice.

These latter two dishes taste entirely unlike each other or their separate ingredients. They are moreover great in nutrition.

ITEM - Boiled rice and raisins.

ITEM - Dish number three with raisins.

ITEM - Rice boiled with raisins, sugar sprinkled on top, and then baked.

ITEM - Ditto with dish number three.

All these are good - and different.

Some people like to cook and have a natural knack for it. Others hate it. If you are one of the former, select a propitious moment to suggest that you will cook, if the rest will wash the dishes and supply the wood and water. Thus you will get first crack at the fire in the chill of morning; and at night you can squat on your heels doing light labor while the others rustle.

In a mountain trip small stout bags for the provisions are necessary. They should be big enough to contain, say, five pounds of corn-meal, and should tie firmly at the top. It will be absolutely labor lost for you to mark them on the outside, as the outside soon will become uniform in color with your marking. Tags might do, if occasionally renewed. But if you have the instinct, you will soon come to recognize the appearance of the different bags as you recognize the features of your family. They should contain small quantities for immediate use of the provisions the main stock of which is carried on another pack-animal. One tin plate apiece and "one to grow on"; the same of tin cups; half a dozen spoons; four knives and forks; a big spoon; two frying-pans; a broiler; a coffee-pot; a Dutch oven; and three light sheet-iron pails to nest in one another was what we carried on this trip. You see, we had horses. Of course in the woods that outfit would be materially reduced.

For the same reason, since we had our carrying done

for us, we took along two flat iron bars about twenty-four inches in length. These, laid across two stones between which the fire had been built, we used to support our cooking-utensils stove-wise. I should never carry a stove. This arrangement is quite as effective, and possesses the added advantage that wood does not have to be cut for it of any definite length. Again, in the woods these iron bars would be a senseless burden. But early you will learn that while it is foolish to carry a single ounce more than will pay in comfort or convenience for its own transportation, it is equally foolish to refuse the comforts or conveniences that modified circumstance will permit you. To carry only a forest equipment with pack-animals would be as silly as to carry only a pack-animal outfit on a Pullman car. Only look out that you do not reverse it.

Even if you do not intend to wash dishes, bring along some "Gold Dust." It is much simpler in getting at odd corners of obstinate kettles than any soap. All you have to do is to boil some of it in that kettle, and the utensil is tamed at once.

That's about all you, as expert cook, are going to need in the way of equipment. Now as to your fire.

There are a number of ways of building a cooking fire, but they share one first requisite: it should be small. A blaze will burn everything, including your hands and your temper. Two logs laid side by side and slanted towards each other so that small things can go on the narrow end and big things on the wide end; flat rocks arranged in the same manner; a narrow trench in which the fire is built; and the flat irons just described - these are the best-known methods. Use dry wood. Arrange to do your boiling first - in the flame; and your frying and broiling last - after the flames have died to coals.

So much in general. You must remember that open-air cooking is in many things quite different from indoor cooking. You have different utensils, are exposed to varying temperatures, are limited in resources, and pursued by a necessity of haste. Pre-conceived notions must go by the board. You are after results; and if you get them, do not mind the feminines of your household lifting the hands of horror over the unorthodox means. Mighty few women I have ever seen were good camp-fire cooks; not because camp-fire cookery is especially difficult, but because they are temperamentally incapable of ridding themselves of the notion that certain things should be done in a certain way, and because if an ingredient lacks, they cannot bring themselves to substitute an approximation. They would rather abandon the dish than do violence to the sacred art.

Most camp-cookery advice is quite useless for the same reason. I have seen many a recipe begin with the words: "Take the yolks of four eggs, half a cup of butter, and a cup of fresh milk - " As if any one really camping in the wilderness ever had eggs, butter, and milk!

Now here is something I cooked for this particular celebration. Every woman to whom I have ever described it has informed me vehemently that it is not cake, and must be "horrid." Perhaps it is not cake, but it looks yellow and light, and tastes like cake.

First I took two cups of flour, and a half cup of corn-meal to make it look yellow. In this I mixed a lot of baking-powder, - about twice what one should use for bread, - and topped off with a cup of sugar. The whole I mixed with water into a light dough. Into the dough went raisins that had previously been boiled to swell them up. Thus was the cake mixed. Now I poured half the dough into the Dutch oven, sprinkled it with a good layer of sugar, cinnamon, and unboiled raisins; poured in the rest of the dough; repeated the layer of sugar, cinnamon, and raisins; and baked in the Dutch oven. It was gorgeous, and we ate it at one fell swoop.

While we are about it, we may as well work backwards on this particular orgy by describing the rest of our dessert. In addition to the cake and some stewed apricots, I, as cook of the day, constructed also a pudding.

The basis was flour - two cups of it. Into this I dumped a handful of raisins, a tablespoonful of baking-powder, two of sugar, and about a pound of fat salt pork cut into little cubes. This I mixed up into a mess by means of a cup or so of water and a quantity of larrupy-dope.[3] Then I dipped a flour-sack in hot water, wrung it out, sprinkled it with dry flour, and half filled it with my pudding mixture. The whole outfit I boiled for two hours in a kettle. It, too, was good to the palate, and was even better sliced and fried the following morning.

[3] Camp-lingo for any kind of syrup.

This brings us to the suspension of kettles. There are two ways. If you are in a hurry, cut a springy pole, sharpen one end, and stick it perpendicular in the ground. Bend it down towards your fire. Hang your kettle on the end of it. If you have jabbed it far enough into the ground in the first place, it will balance nicely by its own spring and the elasticity of the turf. The other method is to plant two forked sticks on either side your fire over which a strong cross-piece is laid. The kettles are hung on hooks cut from forked branches. The forked branches are attached to the cross-piece by means of thongs or withes.

On this occasion we had deer, grouse, and ducks in the larder. The best way to treat them is as follows. You may be sure we adopted the best way.

When your deer is fresh, you will enjoy greatly a dish of liver and bacon. Only the liver you will discover to be a great deal tenderer and more delicate than any calf's liver you ever ate. There is this difference: a deer's liver should be parboiled in order to get rid of a green bitter scum that will rise to the surface and which you must skim off.

Next in order is the "back strap" and tenderloin, which is always tender, even when fresh. The hams should be kept at least five days. Deer-steak, to my notion, is best broiled, though occasionally it is pleasant by way of variety to fry it. In that case a brown gravy is made by thoroughly heating flour in the grease, and then stirring in water. Deer-steak threaded on switches and "barbecued" over the coals is delicious. The outside will be a little blackened, but all the juices will be retained. To enjoy this to the utmost you should take it in your fingers and GNAW. The only permissible implement is your hunting-knife. Do not forget to peel and char slightly the switches on which you thread the meat, otherwise they will impart their fresh-wood taste.

By this time the ribs are in condition. Cut little slits between them, and through the slits thread in and out long strips of bacon. Cut other little gashes, and fill these gashes with onions chopped very fine. Suspend the ribs across two stones between which you have allowed a fire to die down to coals.

There remain now the hams, shoulders, and heart. The two former furnish steaks. The latter you will make into a "bouillon." Here inserts itself quite naturally the philosophy of boiling meat. It may be stated in a paragraph.

If you want boiled meat, put it in hot water. That sets the juices. If you want soup, put it in cold water and bring to a boil. That sets free the juices. Remember this.

Now you start your bouillon cold. Into a kettle of water put your deer hearts, or your fish, a chunk of pork, and some salt. Bring to a boil. Next drop in quartered potatoes, several small whole onions, a half cupful of rice, a can of tomatoes - if you have any. Boil slowly for an hour or so - until things pierce easily under the fork. Add several chunks of bread and a little flour for thickening. Boil down to about a chowder consistency, and serve hot. It is all you will need for that meal; and you will eat of it until there is no more.

I am supposing throughout that you know enough to use salt and pepper when needed.

So much for your deer. The grouse you can split and fry, in which case the brown gravy described for the fried deer-steak is just the thing. Or you can boil him. If you do that, put him into hot water, boil slowly, skim frequently, and add dumplings mixed of flour, baking-powder, and a little lard. Or you can roast him in your Dutch oven with your ducks.

Perhaps it might be well here to explain the Dutch oven. It is a heavy iron kettle with little legs and an iron cover. The theory of it is that coals go among the little legs and on top of the iron cover. This heats the inside, and so cooking results. That, you will observe, is the theory.

In practice you will have to remember a good many things. In the first place, while other affairs are preparing, lay the cover on the fire to heat it through; but not on too hot a place nor too long, lest it warp and so fit loosely. Also the oven itself is to be heated through, and well greased. Your first baking will undoubtedly be burned on the bottom. It is almost impossible without many trials to understand just how little heat suffices underneath. Sometimes it seems that the warmed earth where the fire has been is enough. And on top you do not want a bonfire. A nice even heat, and patience, are the proper ingredients. Nor drop into the error of letting your bread chill, and so fall to unpalatable heaviness. Probably for some time you will alternate between the extremes of heavy crusts with doughy insides, and white weighty boiler-plate with no distinguishable crusts at all. Above all, do not lift the lid too often for the sake of taking a look. Have faith.

There are other ways of baking bread. In the North Country forests, where you carry everything on your back, you will do it in the frying-pan. The mixture should be a rather thick batter or a rather thin dough. It is turned into the frying-pan and baked first on one side, then on the other, the pan being propped on edge facing the fire. The whole secret of success is first to set your pan horizontal and about three feet from the fire in order that the mixture may be thoroughly warmed - not heated - before the pan is propped on edge. Still another way of baking is in a reflector oven of tin. This is highly satisfactory, provided the oven is built on the scientific angles to throw the heat evenly on all parts of the bread-pan and equally on top and bottom. It is not so easy as you might imagine to get a good one made. These reflectors are all right for a permanent camp, but too fragile for transportation on pack-animals.

As for bread, try it unleavened once in a while by way of change. It is really very good, - just salt, water, flour, and a very little sugar. For those who like their bread "all crust," it is especially toothsome. The usual camp bread that I have found the most successful has been in the proportion of two cups of flour to a teaspoonful of salt, one of sugar, and three of baking-powder. Sugar or cinnamon sprinkled on top is sometimes pleasant. Test by thrusting a splinter into the loaf. If dough adheres to the wood, the bread is not done. Biscuits are made by using twice as much baking-powder and about two tablespoonfuls of lard for shortening. They bake much more quickly than the bread. Johnny-cake you mix of corn-meal three cups, flour one cup, sugar four spoonfuls, salt one spoonful, baking-powder four spoonfuls, and lard twice as much as for biscuits. It also is good, very good.

The flapjack is first cousin to bread, very palatable, and extremely indigestible when made of flour, as is ordinarily done. However, the self-raising buckwheat flour makes an excellent flapjack, which is likewise good for your insides. The batter is rather thin, is poured into the piping hot greased pan, "flipped" when

Stewart Edward White

brown on one side, and eaten with larrupy-dope or brown gravy.

When you come to consider potatoes and beans and onions and such matters, remember one thing: that in the higher altitudes water boils at a low temperature, and that therefore you must not expect your boiled food to cook very rapidly. In fact, you'd better leave beans at home. We did. Potatoes you can sometimes tease along by quartering them.

Rolled oats are better than oatmeal. Put them in plenty of water and boil down to the desired consistency. In lack of cream you will probably want it rather soft.

Put your coffee into cold water, bring to a boil, let boil for about two minutes, and immediately set off. Settle by letting a half cup of cold water flow slowly into the pot from the height of a foot or so. If your utensils are clean, you will surely have good coffee by this simple method. Of course you will never boil your tea.

The sun was nearly down when we raised our long yell. The cow-puncher promptly responded. We ate. Then we smoked. Then we basely left all our dishes until the morrow, and followed our cow-puncher to his log cabin, where we were to spend the evening.

By now it was dark, and a bitter cold swooped down from the mountains. We built a fire in a huge stone fireplace and sat around in the flickering light telling ghost-stories to one another. The place was rudely furnished, with only a hard earthen floor, and chairs hewn by the axe. Rifles, spurs, bits, revolvers, branding-irons in turn caught the light and vanished in the shadow. The skin of a bear looked at us from hollow eye-sockets in which there were no eyes. We talked of the Long Trail. Outside the wind, rising, howled through the shakes of the roof.

XV

ON THE WIND AT NIGHT

The winds were indeed abroad that night. They rattled our cabin, they shrieked in our eaves, they puffed down our chimney, scattering the ashes and leaving in the room a balloon of smoke as though a shell had burst. When we opened the door and stepped out, after our good-nights had been said, it caught at our hats and garments as though it had been lying in wait for us.

To our eyes, fire-dazzled, the night seemed very dark. There would be a moon later, but at present even the stars seemed only so many pinpoints of dull metal, lustreless, without illumination. We felt our way to camp, conscious of the softness of grasses, the uncertainty of stones.

At camp the remains of the fire crouched beneath the rating of the storm. Its embers glowed sullen and red, alternately glaring with a half-formed resolution to rebel, and dying to a sulky resignation. Once a feeble flame sprang up for an instant, but was immediately pounced on and beaten flat as though by a vigilant antagonist.

We, stumbling, gathered again our tumbled blankets. Across the brow of the knoll lay a huge pine trunk. In its shelter we respread our bedding, and there, standing, dressed for the night. The power of the wind tugged at our loose garments, hoping for spoil. A towel, shaken by accident from the interior of a sweater, departed white-winged, like a bird, into the outer blackness. We found it next day caught in the bushes several hundred yards distant. Our voices as we shouted were snatched from our lips and hurled lavishly into space. The very breath of our bodies seemed driven back, so that as we faced the elements, we breathed in gasps, with difficulty.

Then we dropped down into our blankets.

At once the prostrate tree-trunk gave us its protection. We lay in a little back-wash of the racing winds, still as a night in June. Over us roared the battle. We felt like sharpshooters in the trenches; as though, were we to raise our heads, at that instant we should enter a zone of danger. So we lay quietly on our backs and stared at the heavens.

The first impression thence given was of stars sailing serene and unaffected, remote from the turbulence of what until this instant had seemed to fill the universe. They were as always, just as we should see them when the evening was warm and the tree-toads chirped clearly audible at half a mile. The importance of the tempest shrank. Then below them next we noticed the mountains; they too were serene and calm.

Immediately it was as though the storm were an hallucination; something not objective; something real, but within the soul of him who looked upon it. It claimed sudden kinship with those blackest days when nevertheless the sun, the mere external unimportant sun, shines with superlative brilliancy. Emotions of a power to shake the foundations of life seemed vaguely to stir in answer to these their hollow symbols. For after all, we were contented at heart and tranquil in mind, and this was but the outer gorgeous show of an intense emotional experience we did not at the moment prove. Our nerves responded to it automatically. We became excited, keyed to a high tension, and so lay rigid on our backs, as though fighting out the battles of our souls.

It was all so unreal and yet so plain to our senses that perforce automatically our experience had to conclude it psychical. We were in air absolutely still. Yet above us the trees writhed and twisted and turned and bent and struck back, evidently in the power of a mighty force. Across the calm heavens the murk of flying atmosphere - I have always maintained that if you looked closely enough you could SEE the wind - the dim, hardly-made-out, fine debris fleeing high in the air; - these faintly hinted at intense movement rushing down through space. A roar of sound filled the hollow of the sky. Occasionally it intermitted, falling abruptly in volume like the mysterious rare hushings of a rapid stream. Then the familiar noises of a summer night became audible for the briefest instant, - a horse sneezed, an owl hooted, the wild call of birds came down the wind. And with a howl the legions of good and evil took up their warring. It was too real, and yet it was not reconcilable with the calm of our resting-places.

For hours we lay thus in all the intensity of an inner storm and stress, which it seemed could not fail to develop us, to mould us, to age us, to leave on us its scars, to bequeath us its peace or remorse or despair, as would some great mysterious dark experience direct from the sources of life. And then abruptly we were exhausted, as we should have been by too great emotion. We fell asleep. The morning dawned still and clear, and garnished and set in order as though such things had never been. Only our white towel fluttered like a flag of truce in the direction the mighty elements had departed.

Stewart Edward White

XVI

THE VALLEY

Once upon a time I happened to be staying in a hotel room which had originally been part of a suite, but which was then cut off from the others by only a thin door through which sounds carried clearly. It was about eleven o'clock in the evening. The occupants of that next room came home. I heard the door open and close. Then the bed shrieked aloud as somebody fell heavily upon it. There breathed across the silence a deep restful sigh.

"Mary," said a man's voice, "I'm mighty sorry I didn't join that Association for Artificial Vacations. They guarantee to get you just as tired and just as mad in two days as you could by yourself in two weeks."

We thought of that one morning as we descended the Glacier Point Trail in Yosemite.

The contrast we need not have made so sharp. We might have taken the regular wagon-road by way of Chinquapin, but we preferred to stick to the trail, and so encountered our first sign of civilization within an hundred yards of the brink. It, the sign, was tourists. They were male and female, as the Lord had made them, but they had improved on that idea since. The women were freckled, hatted with alpines, in which edelweiss - artificial, I think - flowered in abundance; they sported severely plain flannel shirts, bloomers of an aggressive and unnecessary cut, and enormous square boots weighing pounds. The men had on hats just off the sunbonnet effect, pleated Norfolk jackets, bloomers ditto ditto to the women, stockings whose tops rolled over innumerable times to help out the size of that which they should have contained, and also enormous square boots. The female children they put in skin-tight blue overalls. The male children they dressed in bloomers. Why this should be I cannot tell you. All carried toy hatchets with a spike on one end built to resemble the pictures of alpenstocks.

They looked business-like, trod with an assured air of veterans and a seeming of experience more extended than it was possible to pack into any one human life. We stared at them, our eyes bulging out. They painfully and evidently concealed a curiosity as to our pack-train. We wished them good-day, in order to see to what language heaven had fitted their extraordinary ideas as regards raiment. They inquired the way to something or other - I think Sentinel Dome. We had just arrived, so we did not know, but in order to show a friendly spirit we blandly pointed out A way. It may have led to Sentinel Dome for all I know. They departed uttering thanks in human speech.

Now this particular bunch of tourists was evidently staying at the Glacier Point, and so was fresh. But in the course of that morning we descended straight down a drop of, is it four thousand feet? The trail was steep and long and without water. During the descent we passed first and last probably two score of tourists, all on foot. A good half of them were delicate women,

- young, middle-aged, a few gray-haired and evidently upwards of sixty. There were also old men, and fat men, and men otherwise out of condition. Probably nine out of ten, counting in the entire outfit, were utterly unaccustomed, when at home where grow street-cars and hansoms, to even the mildest sort of exercise. They had come into the Valley, whose floor is over four thousand feet up, without the slightest physical preparation for the altitude. They had submitted to the fatigue of a long and dusty stage journey. And then they had merrily whooped it up at a gait which would have appalled seasoned old stagers like ourselves. Those blessed lunatics seemed positively unhappy unless they climbed up to some new point of view every day. I have never seen such a universally tired out, frazzled, vitally exhausted, white-faced, nervous community in my life as I did during our four days' stay in the Valley. Then probably they go away, and take a month to get over it, and have queer residual impressions of the trip. I should like to know what those impressions really are.

Not but that Nature has done everything in her power to oblige them. The things I am about to say are heresy, but I hold them true.

Yosemite is not as interesting nor as satisfying to me as some of the other big box canons, like those of the Tehipite, the Kings in its branches, or the Kaweah. I will admit that its waterfalls are better. Otherwise it possesses no features which are not to be seen in its sister valleys. And there is this difference. In Yosemite everything is jumbled together, apparently for the benefit of the tourist with a linen duster and but three days' time at his disposal. He can turn from the cliff-headland to the dome, from the dome to the half dome, to the glacier formation, the granite slide and all the rest of it, with hardly the necessity of stirring his feet. Nature has put samples of all her works here within reach of his cataloguing vision. Everything is crowded in together, like a row of houses in forty-foot lots. The mere things themselves are here in profusion and wonder, but the appropriate spacing, the approach, the surrounding of subordinate detail which should lead in artistic gradation to the supreme feature - these things, which are a real and essential part of esthetic effect, are lacking utterly for want of room. The place is not natural scenery; it is a junk-shop, a storehouse, a sample-room wherein the elements of natural scenery are to be viewed. It is not an arrangement of effects in accordance with the usual laws of landscape, but an abnormality, a freak of Nature.

All these things are to be found elsewhere. There are cliffs which to the naked eye are as grand as El Capitan; domes, half domes, peaks as noble as any to be seen in the Valley; sheer drops as breath-taking as that from Glacier Point. But in other places each of these is led up to appropriately, and stands the central and satisfying feature to which all other things look. Then you journey on from your cliff, or whatever it happens to be, until, at just the right distance, so that it gains from the presence of its neighbor without losing from its proximity, a dome or a pinnacle takes to itself the right of prominence. I concede the waterfalls; but in other respects I prefer the sister valleys.

That is not to say that one should not visit Yosemite; nor that one will be disappointed. It is grand beyond any possible human belief; and no one, even a nerve-frazzled tourist, can gaze on it without the strongest emotion. Only it is not so intimately satisfying as it should be. It is a show. You do not take it into your heart. "Whew!" you cry. "Isn't that a wonder!" then after a moment, "Looks just like the photographs. Up to sample. Now let's go."

As we descended the trail, we and the tourists aroused in each other a mutual interest. One husband was trying to encourage his young and handsome wife to go on. She was beautifully dressed for the part in a marvelous, becoming costume of whipcord - short skirt, high laced elkskin boots and the rest of it; but in all her magnificence she had sat down on the ground, her back to the cliff, her legs across the trail, and was so tired out that she could hardly muster interest enough to pull them in out of the way of our horses' hoofs. The man inquired anxiously of us how far it was to the top. Now it was a long distance to the top, but a longer to the bottom, so we lied a lie that I am sure was immediately forgiven us, and told them it was only a short climb. I should have offered them the use of Bullet, but Bullet had come far enough, and this was only one of a dozen such cases. In marked contrast was a jolly white-haired clergyman of the bishop type who climbed vigorously and hailed us with a shout.

The horses were decidedly unaccustomed to any such sights, and we sometimes had our hands full getting them by on the narrow way. The trail was safe enough, but it did have an edge, and that edge jumped pretty straight off. It was interesting to observe how the tourists acted. Some of them were perfect fools, and we had more trouble with them than we did with the horses. They could not seem to get the notion into their heads that all we wanted them to do was to get on the inside and stand still. About half of them were terrified to death, so that at the crucial moment, just as a horse was passing them, they had little fluttering panics that called the beast's attention. Most of the remainder tried to be bold and help. They reached out the hand of assistance toward the halter rope; the astonished animal promptly snorted, tried to turn around, cannoned against the next in line. Then there was a mix-up. Two tall clean-cut well-bred looking girls of our slim patrician type offered us material assistance. They seemed to understand horses, and got out of the way in the proper manner, did just the right thing, and made sensible suggestions. I offer them my homage.

They spoke to us as though they had penetrated the disguise of long travel, and could see we were not necessarily members of Burt Alvord's gang. This phase too of our descent became increasingly interesting to us, a species of gauge by which we measured the perceptions of those we encountered. Most did not speak to us at all. Others responded to our greetings with a reserve in which was more than a tinge of distrust. Still others patronized us. A very few overlooked our faded flannel shirts, our soiled trousers, our floppy old hats with their rattlesnake bands, the wear and tear of our equipment, to respond to us heartily. Them in return we generally perceived to belong to our totem.

We found the floor of the Valley well sprinkled with campers. They had pitched all kinds of tents; built all kinds of fancy permanent conveniences; erected all kinds of banners and signs advertising their identity, and were generally having a nice, easy, healthful, jolly kind of a time up there in the mountains. Their outfits they had either brought in with their own wagons, or had had freighted. The store near the bend of the Merced supplied all their needs. It was truly a pleasant sight to see so many people enjoying themselves, for they were mostly those in moderate circumstances to whom a trip on tourist lines would be impossible. We saw bakers' and grocers' and butchers' wagons that had been pressed into service. A man, his wife, and little baby had come in an ordinary buggy, the one horse of which, led by the man, carried the woman and baby to the various points of interest.

We reported to the official in charge, were allotted a camping and grazing place, and proceeded to make ourselves at home.

During the next two days we rode comfortably here and there and looked at things. The things could not be spoiled, but their effect was very materially marred by the swarms of tourists. Sometimes they were silly, and cracked inane and obvious jokes in ridicule of the grandest objects they had come so far to see; some-times they were detestable and left their insignificant calling-cards or their unimportant names where nobody could ever have any object in reading them; sometimes they were pathetic and helpless and had to have assistance; sometimes they were amusing; hardly ever did they seem entirely human. I wonder what there is about the traveling public that seems so to set it apart, to make of it at least a sub-species of mankind?

Among other things, we were vastly interested in the guides. They were typical of this sort of thing. Each morning one of these men took a pleasantly awe-stricken band of tourists out, led them around in the brush awhile, and brought them back in time for lunch. They wore broad hats and leather bands and exotic raiment and fierce expressions, and looked dark and mysterious and extra-competent over the most trivial of difficulties.

Nothing could be more instructive than to see two or three of these imitation bad men starting out in the morning to "guide" a flock, say to Nevada Falls. The tourists, being about to mount, have outdone themselves in weird and awesome clothes – especially the women. Nine out of ten wear their stirrups too short, so their knees are hunched up. One guide rides at the head - great deal of silver spur, clanking chain, and the rest of it. Another rides in the rear. The third rides up and down the line, very gruff, very preoccupied, very careworn over the dangers of the way. The cavalcade moves. It proceeds for about a mile. There arise sudden cries, great but subdued excitement. The leader stops, raising a commanding hand. Guide number three gallops up. There is a consultation. The cinch-strap of the brindle shave-tail is taken up two inches. A catastrophe has been averted. The noble three look volumes of relief. The cavalcade moves again.

Now the trail rises. It is a nice, safe, easy trail. But to the tourists it is made terrible. The noble three see to that. They pass more dangers by the exercise of superhuman skill than you or I could discover in a summer's close search. The joke of the matter is that those forty-odd saddle-animals have been over that trail so many times that one would have difficulty in heading them off from it once they got started.

Very much the same criticism would hold as to the popular notion of the Yosemite stage-drivers. They drive well, and seem efficient men. But their wonderful reputation would have to be upheld on rougher roads than those into the Valley. The tourist is, of course, encouraged to believe that he is doing the hair-breadth escape; but in reality, as mountain travel goes, the Yosemite stage-road is very mild.

This that I have been saying is not by way of depreciation. But it seems to me that the Valley is wonderful enough to stand by itself in men's appreciation without the unreality of sickly sentimentalism in regard to imaginary dangers, or the histrionics of playing wilderness where no wilderness exists.

As we went out, this time by the Chinquapin wagon-road, we met one stage-load after another of tourists coming in. They had not yet donned the outlandish attire they believe proper to the occasion, and so showed for what they were, - prosperous, well-bred, well-dressed travelers. In contrast to their smartness, the brilliancy of new-painted stages, the dash of the horses maintained by the Yosemite Stage Company, our own dusty travel-worn outfit of mountain ponies, our own rough clothes patched and faded, our sheath-knives and firearms seemed out of place and curious, as though a knight in medieval armor were to ride down Broadway.

I do not know how many stages there were. We turned our pack-horses out for them all, dashing back and forth along the line, coercing the diabolical Dinkey. The road was too smooth. There were no obstructions to surmount; no dangers to avert; no difficulties to avoid. We could not get into trouble, but proceeded as on a county turnpike. Too tame, too civilized, too representative of the tourist element, it ended by getting on our nerves. The wilderness seemed to have left us forever. Never would we get back to our own again. After a long time Wes, leading, turned into our old trail branching off to the high country. Hardly had we traveled a half mile before we heard from the advance guard a crash and a shout.

"What is it, Wes?" we yelled.

In a moment the reply came, -

"Lily's fallen down again, - thank God!"

We understood what he meant. By this we knew that the tourist zone was crossed, that we had left the show country, and were once more in the open.

XVII

THE MAIN CREST

The traveler in the High Sierras generally keeps to the west of the main crest. Sometimes he approaches fairly to the foot of the last slope; sometimes he angles away and away even down to what finally seems to him a lower country, - to the pine mountains of only five or six thousand feet. But always to the left or right of him, according to whether he travels south or north, runs the rampart of the system, sometimes glittering with snow, sometimes formidable and rugged with splinters and spires of granite. He crosses spurs and tributary ranges as high, as rugged, as snow-clad as these. They do not quite satisfy him. Over beyond he thinks he ought to see something great, - some wide outlook, some space bluer than his trail can offer him. One day or another he clamps his decision, and so turns aside for the simple and only purpose of standing on the top of the world.

We were bitten by that idea while crossing the Granite Basin. The latter is some ten thousand feet in the air, a cup of rock five or six miles across, surrounded by mountains much higher than itself. That would have been sufficient for most moods, but, resting on the edge of a pass ten thousand six hundred feet high, we concluded that we surely would have to look over into Nevada.

We got out the map. It became evident, after a little study, that by descending six thousand feet into a box canon, proceeding in it a few miles, and promptly climbing out again, by climbing steadily up the long narrow course of another box canon for about a day and a half's journey, and then climbing out of that to a high ridge country with little flat valleys, we would come to a wide lake in a meadow eleven thousand feet up. There we could camp. The mountain opposite was thirteen thousand three hundred and twenty feet, so the climb from the lake became merely a matter of computation. This, we figured, would take us just a week, which may seem a considerable time to sacrifice to the gratification of a whim. But such a glorious whim!

We descended the great box canon, and scaled its upper end, following near the voices of a cascade. Cliffs thousands of feet high hemmed us in. At the very top of them strange crags leaned out looking down on us in the abyss. From a projection a colossal sphinx gazed solemnly across at a dome as smooth and symmetrical as, but vastly larger than, St. Peter's at Rome.

The trail labored up to the brink of the cascade. At once we entered a long narrow aisle between regular palisaded cliffs.

The formation was exceedingly regular. At the top the precipice fell sheer for a thousand feet or so; then the steep slant of the debris, like buttresses, down almost to the bed of the river. The lower parts of the buttresses were clothed with heavy chaparral, which, nearer moisture, developed into cottonwoods,alders, tangled vines, flowers, rank grasses. And away on the very edge of the cliffs, close under the sky, were pines, belittled by distance, solemn and aloof, like Indian warriors wrapped in their blankets watching from an eminence the passage of a hostile force.

We caught rainbow trout in the dashing white torrent of the river. We followed the trail through delicious thickets redolent with perfume; over the roughest granite slides, along still dark aisles of forest groves, between the clefts of boulders so monstrous as almost to seem an insult to the credulity. Among the chaparral, on the slope of the buttress across the river, we made out a bear feeding. Wes and I sat ten minutes waiting for him to show sufficiently for a chance. Then we took a shot at about four hundred yards, and hit him somewhere so he angled down the hill furiously. We left the Tenderfoot to watch that he did not come out of the big thicket of the river bottom where last we had seen him, while we scrambled upstream nearly a mile looking for a way across. Then we trailed him by the blood, each step one of suspense, until we fairly had to crawl in after him; and shot him five times more, three in the head, before he gave up not six feet from us; and shouted gloriously and skinned that bear. But the meat was badly bloodshot, for there were three bullets in the head, two in the chest and shoulders, one through the paunch, and one in the hind quarters.

Since we were much in want of meat, this grieved us. But that noon while we ate, the horses ran down toward us, and wheeled, as though in cavalry formation, looking toward the hill and snorting. So I put down my tin plate gently, and took up my rifle, and without rising shot that bear through the back of the neck. We took his skin, and also his hind quarters, and went on.

By the third day from Granite Basin we reached the end of the long narrow canon with the high cliffs and the dark pine-trees and the very blue sky. Therefore we turned sharp to the left and climbed laboriously until we had come up into the land of big boulders, strange spare twisted little trees, and the singing of the great wind.

The country here was mainly of granite. It out- cropp-ed in dikes, it slid down the slopes in aprons, it strewed the prospect in boulders and blocks, it seamed the hollows with knife-ridges. Soil gave the impression of having been laid on top; you divined the granite beneath it, and not so very far beneath it, either. A fine hair-grass grew close to this soil, as though to produce as many blades as possible in the limited area.

But strangest of all were the little thick twisted trees with the rich shaded umber color of their trunks. They occurred rarely, but still in sufficient regularity to lend the impression of a scattered grove-cohesiveness. Their limbs were sturdy and reaching fantastically. On each trunk the colors ran in streaks, patches, and gradations from a sulphur yellow, through browns and red-orange, to a rich red-umber. They were like the earth-dwarfs of German legend, come out to view the roof of their workshop in the interior of the hill; or, more subtly, like some of the more fantastic engravings of Gustave Dore.

We camped that night at a lake whose banks were pebbled in the manner of an artificial pond, and whose setting was a thin meadow of the fine hair-grass, for

Stewart Edward White

the grazing of which the horses had to bare their teeth. All about, the granite mountains rose. The timber-line, even of the rare shrub-like gnome-trees, ceased here. Above us was nothing whatever but granite rock, snow, and the sky.

It was just before dusk, and in the lake the fish were jumping eagerly. They took the fly well, and before the fire was alight we had caught three for supper. When I say we caught but three, you will understand that they were of good size. Firewood was scarce, but we dragged in enough by means of Old Slob and a riata to build us a good fire. And we needed it, for the cold descended on us with the sharpness and vigor of eleven thousand feet.

For such an altitude the spot was ideal. The lake just below us was full of fish. A little stream ran from it by our very elbows. The slight elevation was level, and covered with enough soil to offer a fairly good substructure for our beds. The flat in which was the lake reached on up narrower and narrower to the foot of the last slope, furnishing for the horses an admirable natural corral about a mile long. And the view was magnificent.

First of all there were the mountains above us, towering grandly serene against the sky of morning; then all about us the tumultuous slabs and boulders and blocks of granite among which dare-devil and hardy little trees clung to a footing as though in defiance of some great force exerted against them; then below us a sheer drop, into which our brook plunged, with its suggestion of depths; and finally beyond those depths the giant peaks of the highest Sierras rising lofty as the sky, shrouded in a calm and stately peace.

Next day the Tenderfoot and I climbed to the top. Wes decided at the last minute that he hadn't lost any mountains, and would prefer to fish.

The ascent was accompanied by much breathlessness and a heavy pounding of our hearts, so that we were forced to stop every twenty feet to recover our physical balance. Each step upward dragged at our feet like a leaden weight. Yet once we were on the level, or once we ceased our very real exertions for a second or so, the difficulty left us, and we breathed as easily as in the lower altitudes.

The air itself was of a quality impossible to describe to you unless you have traveled in the high countries. I know it is trite to say that it had the exhilaration of wine, yet I can find no better simile. We shouted and whooped and breathed deep and wanted to do things.

The immediate surroundings of that mountain peak were absolutely barren and absolutely still. How it was accomplished so high up I do not know, but the entire structure on which we moved - I cannot say walked - was composed of huge granite slabs. Sometimes these were laid side by side like exaggerated paving flags; but oftener they were up-ended, piled in a confusion over which we had precariously to scramble. And the silence. It was so still that the very ringing in our ears came to a prominence absurd and almost terrifying. The wind swept by noiseless, because it had nothing movable to startle into noise. The solid eternal granite lay heavy in its statics across the possibility of even a whisper. The blue vault of heaven seemed emptied of sound.

But the wind did stream by unceasingly, weird in the

Stewart Edward White

unaccustomedness of its silence. And the sky was blue as a turquoise, and the sun burned fiercely, and the air was cold as the water of a mountain spring.

We stretched ourselves behind a slab of granite, and ate the luncheon we had brought, cold venison steak and bread. By and by a marvelous thing happened. A flash of wings sparkled in the air, a brave little voice challenged us cheerily, a pert tiny rock-wren flirted his tail and darted his wings and wanted to know what we were thinking of anyway to enter his especial territory. And shortly from nowhere appeared two Canada Jays, silent as the wind itself, hoping for a share in our meal. Then the Tenderfoot discovered in a niche some strange, hardy alpine flowers. So we established a connection, through these wondrous brave children of the great mother, with the world of living things.

After we had eaten, which was the very first thing we did, we walked to the edge of the main crest and looked over. That edge went straight down. I do not know how far, except that even in contemplation we entirely lost our breaths, before we had fallen half way to the bottom. Then intervened a ledge, and in the ledge was a round glacier lake of the very deepest and richest ultramarine you can find among your paint-tubes, and on the lake floated cakes of dazzling white ice. That was enough for the moment.

Next we leaped at one bound direct down to some brown hazy liquid shot with the tenderest filaments of white. After analysis we discovered the hazy brown liquid to be the earth of the plains, and the filaments of white to be roads. Thus instructed we made out specks which were towns. That was all.

The rest was too insignificant to classify without the aid of a microscope.

And afterwards, across those plains, oh, many, many leagues, were the Inyo and Panamit mountains, and beyond them Nevada and Arizona, and blue mountains, and bluer, and still bluer rising, rising, rising higher and higher until at the level of the eye they blended with the heavens and were lost somewhere away out beyond the edge of the world.

We said nothing, but looked for a long time. Then we turned inland to the wonderful great titans of mountains clear-cut in the crystalline air. Never was such air. Crystalline is the only word which will describe it, for almost it seemed that it would ring clearly when struck, so sparkling and delicate and fragile was it. The crags and fissures across the way - two miles across the way - were revealed through it as through some medium whose transparence was absolute. They challenged the eye, stereoscopic in their relief. Were it not for the belittling effects of the distance, we felt that we might count the frost seams or the glacial scorings on every granite apron. Far below we saw the irregular outline of our lake. It looked like a pond a few hundred feet down. Then we made out a pin-point of white moving leisurely near its border. After a while we realized that the pin-point of white was one of our pack-horses, and immediately the flat little scene shot backwards as though moved from behind and acknowledged its due number of miles. The miniature crags at its back became gigantic; the peaks beyond grew thousands of feet in the establishment of a proportion which the lack of "atmosphere" had denied. We never succeeded in getting adequate photographs. As well take pictures of any eroded little arroyo or granite canon. Relative sizes do not exist, unless pointed out.

"See that speck there?" we explain. "That's a big pine-tree. So by that you can see how tremendous those cliffs really are."

And our guest looks incredulously at the speck.

There was snow, of course, lying cold in the hot sun. This phenomenon always impresses a man when first he sees it. Often I have ridden with my sleeves rolled up and the front of my shirt open, over drifts whose edges, even, dripped no water. The direct rays seem to have absolutely no effect. A scientific explanation I have never heard expressed; but I suppose the cold nights freeze the drifts and pack them so hard that the short noon heat cannot penetrate their density. I may be quite wrong as to my reason, but I am entirely correct as to my fact.

Another curious thing is that we met our mosquitoes only rarely below the snow-line. The camping in the Sierras is ideal for lack of these pests. They never bite hard nor stay long even when found. But just as sure as we approached snow, then we renewed acquaintance with our old friends of the north woods.

It is analogous to the fact that the farther north you go into the fur countries, the more abundant they become.

By and by it was time to descend. The camp lay directly below us. We decided to go to it straight, and so stepped off on an impossibly steep slope covered, not with the great boulders and granite blocks, but with a fine loose shale. At every stride we stepped ten feet and slid five. It was gloriously near to flying. Leaning far back, our arms spread wide to keep our balance, spying alertly far ahead as to where we were going to land, utterly unable to check until we encountered a half-buried ledge of some sort, and shouting wildly at every plunge, we fairly shot downhill. The floor of our valley rose to us as the earth to a descending balloon. In three quarters of an hour we had reached the first flat.

There we halted to puzzle over the trail of a mountain lion clearly printed on the soft ground. What had the great cat been doing away up there above the hunting country, above cover, above everything that would appeal to a well-regulated cat of any size whatsoever? We theorized at length, but gave it up finally, and went on. Then a familiar perfume rose to our nostrils. We plucked curiously at a bed of catnip and wondered whether the animal had journeyed so far to enjoy what is always such a treat to her domestic sisters.

It was nearly dark when we reached camp. We found Wes contentedly scraping away at the bearskins.

"Hello," said he, looking up with a grin. "Hello, you dam fools! I'VE been having a good time. I've been fishing."

XVIII

THE GIANT FOREST

Every one is familiar, at least by reputation and photograph, with the Big Trees of California. All have seen pictures of stage-coaches driving in passageways cut through the bodies of the trunks; of troops of cavalry ridden on the prostrate trees. No one but has heard of the dancing-floor or the dinner-table cut from a single cross-section; and probably few but have seen some of the fibrous bark of unbelievable thickness. The Mariposa, Calaveras, and Santa Cruz groves have become household names.

The public at large, I imagine, meaning by that you and me and our neighbors, harbor an idea that the Big Tree occurs only as a remnant, in scattered little groves carefully fenced and piously visited by the tourist. What would we have said to the information that in the very heart of the Sierras there grows a thriving forest of these great trees; that it takes over a day to ride throughout that forest; and that it comprises probably over five thousand specimens?

Yet such is the case. On the ridges and high plateaus north of the Kaweah River is the forest I describe; and of that forest the trees grow from fifteen to twenty-six feet in diameter. Do you know what that means? Get up from your chair and pace off the room you are in. If it is a very big room, its longest dimension would just about contain one of the bigger trunks. Try to imagine a tree like that.

It must be a columnar tree straight and true as the supports of a Greek facade. The least deviation from the perpendicular of such a mass would cause it to fall. The limbs are sturdy like the arms of Hercules, and grow out from the main trunk direct instead of dividing and leading that main trunk to themselves, as is the case with other trees. The column rises with a true taper to its full height; then is finished with the conical effect of the top of a monument. Strangely enough the frond is exceedingly fine, and the cones small.

When first you catch sight of a Sequoia, it does not impress you particularly except as a very fine tree. Its proportions are so perfect that its effect is rather to belittle its neighbors than to show in its true magnitude. Then, gradually, as your experience takes cognizance of surroundings, - the size of a sugar-pine, of a boulder, of a stream flowing near, - the giant swells and swells before your very vision until he seems at the last even greater than the mere statistics of his inches had led you to believe. And after that first surprise over finding the Sequoia something not monstrous but beautiful in proportion has given place to the full realization of what you are beholding, you will always wonder why no one who has seen has ever given any one who has not seen an adequate idea of these magnificent old trees.

Perhaps the most insistent note, besides that of mere size and dignity, is of absolute stillness. These trees do not sway to the wind, their trunks are constructed to stand solid. Their branches do not bend and murmur, for they too are rigid in fiber. Their fine thread-like needles may catch the breeze's whisper, may draw together and apart for the exchange of confidences as do the leaves of other trees, but if so, you and I are too far below to distinguish it. All about, the other forest growths may be rustling and bowing and singing with the voices of the air; the Sequoia stands in the hush of an absolute calm. It is as though he dreamed, too wrapt in still great thoughts of his youth, when the earth itself was young, to share the worldlier joys of his neighbor, to be aware of them, even himself to breathe deeply. You feel in the presence of these trees as you would feel in the presence of a kindly and benignant sage, too occupied with larger things to enter fully into your little affairs, but well disposed in the wisdom of clear spiritual insight.

This combination of dignity, immobility, and a certain serene detachment has on me very much the same effect as does a mountain against the sky. It is quite unlike the impression made by any other tree, however large, and is lovable.

We entered the Giant Forest by a trail that climbed. Always we entered desirable places by trails that climbed or dropped. Our access to paradise was never easy. About halfway up we met five pack-mules and two men coming down. For some reason, unknown, I suspect, even to the god of chance, our animals behaved themselves and walked straight ahead in a beautiful dignity, while those weak-minded mules scattered and bucked and scraped under trees and dragged back on their halters when caught. The two men cast on us malevolent glances as often as they were able, but spent most of their time swearing and running about. We helped them once or twice by heading off, but were too thankfully engaged in treading lightly over our own phenomenal peace to pay much attention. Long after we had gone on, we caught bursts of rumpus ascending from below. Shortly we came to a comparatively level country, and a little meadow, and a rough sign which read

"Feed 20C a night."

Just beyond this extortion was the Giant Forest.

We entered it toward the close of the afternoon, and rode on after our wonted time looking for feed at less than twenty cents a night. The great trunks, fluted like marble columns, blackened against the western sky. As they grew huger, we seemed to shrink, until we moved fearful as prehistoric man must have moved among the forces over which he had no control. We discovered our feed in a narrow "stringer" a few miles on. That night, we, pigmies, slept in the setting before which should have stridden the colossi of another age. Perhaps eventually, in spite of its magnificence and wonder, we were a little glad to leave the Giant Forest. It held us too rigidly to a spiritual standard of which our normal lives were incapable; it insisted on a loftiness of soul, a dignity, an aloofness from the ordinary affairs of life, the ordinary occupations of thought hardly compatible with the powers of any creature less noble, less aged, less wise in the passing of centuries than itself.

Stewart Edward White

XIX

ON COWBOYS

Your cowboy is a species variously subdivided. If you happen to be traveled as to the wild countries, you will be able to recognize whence your chance acquaintance hails by the kind of saddle he rides, and the rigging of it; by the kind of rope he throws, and the method of the throwing; by the shape of hat he wears; by his twist of speech; even by the very manner of his riding. Your California "vaquero" from the Coast Ranges is as unlike as possible to your Texas cowman, and both differ from the Wyoming or South Dakota article. I should be puzzled to define exactly the habitat of the "typical" cowboy. No matter where you go, you will find your individual acquaintance varying from the type in respect to some of the minor details.

Certain characteristics run through the whole tribe, however. Of these some are so well known or have been so adequately done elsewhere that it hardly seems wise to elaborate on them here. Let us assume that you and I know what sort of human beings cowboys are, - with all their taciturnity, their surface gravity, their keen sense of humor, their courage, their kindness, their freedom, their lawlessness, their foulness of mouth, and their supreme skill in the handling of horses and cattle. I shall try to tell you nothing of all that.

If one thinks down doggedly to the last analysis, he will find that the basic reason for the differences between a cowboy and other men rests finally on an individual liberty, a freedom from restraint either of society or convention, a lawlessness, an accepting of his own standard alone. He is absolutely self-poised and sufficient; and that self-poise and that sufficiency he takes pains to assure first of all. After their assurance he is willing to enter into human relations. His attitude toward everything in life is, not suspicious, but watchful. He is "gathered together," his elbows at his side.

This evidences itself most strikingly in his terseness of speech. A man dependent on himself naturally does not give himself away to the first comer. He is more interested in finding out what the other fellow is than in exploiting his own importance. A man who does much promiscuous talking he is likely to despise, arguing that man incautious, hence weak.

Yet when he does talk, he talks to the point and with a vivid and direct picturesqueness of phrase which is as refreshing as it is unexpected. The delightful remodeling of the English language in Mr. Alfred Lewis's "Wolfville" is exaggerated only in quantity, not in quality. No cowboy talks habitually in quite as original a manner as Mr. Lewis's Old Cattleman; but I have no doubt that in time he would be heard to say all the good things in that volume. I myself have note-books full of just such gorgeous language, some of the best of which I have used elsewhere, and so will not repeat here.[4]

[4] See especially Jackson Himes in The Blazed Trail; and TheRawhide.

This vividness manifests itself quite as often in the selection of the apt word as in the construction of elaborate phrases with a half-humorous intention. A cowboy once told me of the arrival of a tramp by saying, "He SIFTED into camp." Could any verb be more expressive? Does not it convey exactly the lazy, careless, out-at-heels shuffling gait of the hobo? Another in the course of description told of a saloon scene, "They all BELLIED UP TO the bar." Again, a range cook, objecting to purposeless idling about his fire, shouted: "If you fellows come MOPING around here any more, I'LL SURE MAKE YOU HARD TO CATCH!" "Fish in that pond, son? Why, there's some fish in there big enough to rope," another advised me. "I quit shoveling," one explained the story of his life, "because I couldn't see nothing ahead of shoveling but dirt." The same man described ploughing as, "Looking at a mule's tail all day." And one of the most succinct epitomes of the motifs of fiction was offered by an old fellow who looked over my shoulder as I was reading a novel. "Well, son," said he, "what they doing now, KISSING OR KILLING?"

Nor are the complete phrases behind in aptness. I have space for only a few examples, but they will illustrate what I mean. Speaking of a companion who was "putting on too much dog," I was informed, "He walks like a man with a new suit of WOODEN UNDERWEAR!" Or again, in answer to my inquiry as to a mutual acquaintance, "Jim? Oh, poor old Jim! For the last week or so he's been nothing but an insignificant atom of humanity hitched to a boil."

But to observe the riot of imagination turned loose with the bridle off, you must assist at a burst of anger on the part of one of these men. It is mostly unprintable, but you will get an entirely new idea of what profanity means. Also you will come to the conclusion that you, with your trifling DAMNS, and the like, have been a very good boy indeed. The remotest, most obscure, and unheard of conceptions are dragged forth from earth, heaven, and hell, and linked together in a sequence so original, so gaudy, and so utterly blasphemous, that you gasp and are stricken with the most devoted admiration. It is genius.

Of course I can give you no idea here of what these truly magnificent oaths are like. It is a pity, for it would liberalize your education. Occasionally, like a trickle of clear water into an alkali torrent, a straight English sentence will drop into the flood. It is refreshing by contrast, but weak.

"If your brains were all made of dynamite, you couldn't blow the top of your head off."

"I wouldn't speak to him if I met him in hell carrying a lump of ice in his hand."

"That little horse'll throw you so high the black-birds will build nests in your hair before you come down."

These are ingenious and amusing, but need the blazing settings from which I have ravished them to give them their due force.

In Arizona a number of us were sitting around the feeble camp-fire the desert scarcity of fuel permits, smoking our pipes. We were all contemplative and comfortably silent with the exception of one very youthful person who had a lot to say. It was mainly about himself. After he had bragged awhile without molestation, one of the older cow-punchers grew very tired of it. He removed his pipe deliberately, and spat in the fire.

"Say, son," he drawled, "if you want to say something big, why don't you say `elephant'?"

The young fellow subsided. We went on smoking our pipes.

Down near the Chiracahua Range in southeastern Arizona, there is a butte, and halfway up that butte is a cave, and in front of that cave is a ramshackle porch-roof or shed. This latter makes the cave into a dwelling-house. It is inhabited by an old "alkali" and half a dozen bear dogs. I sat with the old fellow one day for nearly an hour. It was a sociable visit, but economical of the English language. He made one remark, outside our initial greeting. It was enough, for in terseness, accuracy, and compression, I have never heard a better or more comprehensive description of the arid countries.

"Son," said he, "in this country thar is more cows and less butter, more rivers and less water, and you kin see farther and see less than in any other country in the world."

Now this peculiar directness of phrase means but one thing, - freedom from the influence of convention. The cowboy respects neither the dictionary nor usage. He employs his words in the manner that best suits him, and arranges them in the sequence that best expresses his idea, untrammeled by tradition. It is a phase of the same lawlessness, the same reliance on self, that makes for his taciturnity and watchfulness.

In essence, his dress is an adaptation to the necessities of his calling; as a matter of fact, it is an elaboration on that. The broad heavy felt hat he has found by experience to be more effective in turning heat than a lighter straw; he further runs to variety in the shape of the crown and in the nature of the band. He wears a silk handkerchief about his neck to turn the sun and keep out the dust, but indulges in astonishing gaudiness of color. His gauntlets save his hands from the rope; he adds a fringe and a silver star. The heavy wide "chaps" of leather about his legs are necessary to him when he is riding fast through brush; he indulges in such frivolities as stamped leather, angora hair, and the like. High heels to his boots prevent his foot from slipping through his wide stirrup, and are useful to dig into the ground when he is roping in the corral. Even his six-shooter is more a tool of his trade than a weapon of defense. With it he frightens cattle from the heavy brush; he slaughters old or diseased steers; he "turns the herd" in a stampede or when rounding it in; and especially is it handy and loose to his hip in case his horse should fall and commence to drag him.

So the details of his appearance spring from the practical, but in the wearing of them and the using of them he shows again that fine disregard for the way other people do it or think it.

Now in civilization you and I entertain a double respect for firearms and the law. Firearms are dangerous, and it is against the law to use them promiscuously. If we shoot them off in unexpected places, we

Stewart Edward White

first of all alarm unduly our families and neighbors, and in due course attract the notice of the police. By the time we are grown up we look on shooting a revolver as something to be accomplished after an especial trip for the purpose.

But to the cowboy shooting a gun is merely what lighting a match would be to us. We take reasonable care not to scratch that match on the wall nor to throw it where it will do harm. Likewise the cowboy takes reasonable care that his bullets do not land in some one's anatomy nor in too expensive bric-a-brac. Otherwise any time or place will do.

The picture comes to me of a bunk-house on an Arizona range. The time was evening. A half-dozen cowboys were sprawled out on the beds smoking, and three more were playing poker with the Chinese cook. A misguided rat darted out from under one of the beds and made for the empty fireplace. He finished his journey in smoke. Then the four who had shot slipped their guns back into their holsters and resumed their cigarettes and drawling low-toned conversation.

On another occasion I stopped for noon at the Circle I ranch. While waiting for dinner, I lay on my back in the bunk-room and counted three hundred and sixty-two bullet-holes in the ceiling. They came to be there because the festive cowboys used to while away the time while lying as I was lying, waiting for supper, in shooting the flies that crawled about the plaster.

This beautiful familiarity with the pistol as a parlor toy accounts in great part for a cowboy's propensity to "shoot up the town" and his indignation when arrested therefor.

The average cowboy is only a fair target-shot with the revolver. But he is chain lightning at getting his gun off in a hurry. There are exceptions to this, however, especially among the older men. Some can handle the Colts 45 and its heavy recoil with almost uncanny accuracy. I have seen individuals who could from their saddles nip lizards darting across the road; and one who was able to perforate twice before it hit the ground a tomato-can tossed into the air. The cowboy is prejudiced against the double-action gun, for some reason or other. He manipulates his single-action weapon fast enough, however.

His sense of humor takes the same unexpected slants, not because his mental processes differ from those of other men, but because he is unshackled by the subtle and unnoticed nothingnesses of precedent which deflect our action toward the common uniformity of our neighbors. It must be confessed that his sense of humor possesses also a certain robustness.

The J. H. outfit had been engaged for ten days in busting broncos. This the Chinese cook, Sang, a newcomer in the territory, found vastly amusing. He liked to throw the ropes off the prostrate broncos, when all was ready; to slap them on the flanks; to yell shrill Chinese yells; and to dance in celestial delight when the terrified animal arose and scattered out of there. But one day the range men drove up a little bunch of full-grown cattle that had been bought from a smaller owner. It was necessary to change the brands. Therefore a little fire was built, the stamp-brand put in to heat, and two of the men on horseback caught a cow by the horns and one hind leg, and promptly upset her. The old brand was obliterated, the new one burnt in. This irritated the cow. Promptly the branding-men, who were of course afoot, climbed to the top of the corral to be out of the way. At this moment, before the horsemen could flip loose their ropes, Sang appeared.

"Hol' on!" he babbled. "I take him off;" and he scrambled over the fence and approached the cow.

Now cattle of any sort rush at the first object they see after getting to their feet. But whereas a steer makes a blind run and so can be avoided, a cow keeps her eyes open. Sang approached that wild-eyed cow, a bland smile on his countenance.

A dead silence fell. Looking about at my companions' faces I could not discern even in the depths of their eyes a single faint flicker of human interest.

Sang loosened the rope from the hind leg, he threw it from the horns, he slapped the cow with his hat, and uttered the shrill Chinese yell. So far all was according to programme.

The cow staggered to her feet, her eyes blazin g fire. She took one good look, and then started for Sang.

What followed occurred with all the briskness of a tune from a circus band. Sang darted for the corral fence. Now, three sides of the corral were railed, and so climbable, but the fourth was a solid adobe wall. Of course Sang went for the wall. There, finding his nails would not stick, he fled down the length of it, his queue streaming, his eyes popping, his talons curved toward an ideal of safety, gibbering strange monkey talk, pursued a scant arm's length behind by that infuriated cow. Did any one help him? Not any. Every man of that crew was hanging weak from laughter to the horn of his saddle or the top of the fence. The preternatural solemnity had broken to little bits. Men came running from the bunk-house, only to go into spasms outside, to roll over and over on the ground, clutching handfuls of herbage in the agony of their delight.

At the end of the corral was a narrow chute. Into this Sang escaped as into a burrow. The cow came too. Sang, in desperation, seized a pole, but the cow dashed such a feeble weapon aside. Sang caught sight of a little opening, too small for cows, back into the main corral. He squeezed through. The cow crashed through after him, smashing the boards. At the crucial moment Sang tripped and fell on his face. The cow missed him by so close a margin that for a moment we thought she had hit. But she had not, and before she could turn, Sang had topped the fence and was halfway to the kitchen. Tom Waters always maintained that he spread his Chinese sleeves and flew. Shortly after a tremendous smoke arose from the kitchen chimney. Sang had gone back to cooking.

Now that Mongolian was really in great danger, but no one of the outfit thought for a moment of any but the humorous aspect of the affair. Analogously, in a certain small cow-town I happened to be transient when the postmaster shot a Mexican. Nothing was done about it. The man went right on being postmaster, but he had to set up the drinks because he had hit the Mexican in the stomach. That was considered a poor place to hit a man.

The entire town of Willcox knocked off work for nearly a day to while away the tedium of an enforced wait there on my part. They wanted me to go fishing.

One man offered a team, the other a saddle-horse. All expended much eloquence in directing me accurately, so that I should be sure to find exactly the spot where I could hang my feet over a bank beneath which there were "a plumb plenty of fish." Somehow or other they raked out miscellaneous tackle. But they were a little too eager. I excused myself and hunted up a map. Sure enough the lake was there, but it had been dry since a previous geological period. The fish were undoubtedly there too, but they were fossil fish. I borrowed a pickaxe and shovel and announced myself as ready to start.

Outside the principal saloon in one town hung a gong. When a stranger was observed to enter the saloon, that gong was sounded. Then it behooved him to treat those who came in answer to the summons.

But when it comes to a case of real hospitality or helpfulness, your cowboy is there every time. You are welcome to food and shelter without price, whether he is at home or not. Only it is etiquette to leave your name and thanks pinned somewhere about the place. Otherwise your intrusion may be considered in the light of a theft, and you may be pursued accordingly.

Contrary to general opinion, the cowboy is not a dangerous man to those not looking for trouble. There are occasional exceptions, of course, but they belong to the universal genus of bully, and can be found among any class. Attend to your own business, be cool and good-natured, and your skin is safe. Then when it is really "up to you," be a man; you will never lack for friends.

The Sierras, especially towards the south where the

meadows are wide and numerous, are full of cattle in small bands. They come up from the desert about the first of June, and are driven back again to the arid countries as soon as the autumn storms begin. In the very high land they are few, and to be left to their own devices; but now we entered a new sort of country.

Below Farewell Gap and the volcanic regions one's surroundings change entirely. The meadows become high flat valleys, often miles in extent; the mountains - while registering big on the aneroid - are so little elevated above the plateaus that a few thousand feet is all of their apparent height; the passes are low, the slopes easy, the trails good, the rock outcrops few, the hills grown with forests to their very tops. Altogether it is a country easy to ride through, rich in grazing, cool and green, with its eight thousand feet of elevation. Consequently during the hot months thousands of desert cattle are pastured here; and with them come many of the desert men.

Our first intimation of these things was in the volcanic region where swim the golden trout. From the advantage of a hill we looked far down to a hair-grass meadow through which twisted tortuously a brook, and by the side of the brook, belittled by distance, was a miniature man. We could see distinctly his every movement, as he approached cautiously the stream's edge, dropped his short line at the end of a stick over the bank, and then yanked bodily the fish from beneath. Behind him stood his pony. We could make out in the clear air the coil of his raw-hide "rope," the glitter of his silver bit, the metal points on his saddle skirts, the polish of his six-shooter, the gleam of his fish, all the details of his costume. Yet he was fully a mile distant. After a time he picked up his string of fish, mounted, and jogged loosely away at the cow-pony's little Spanish trot toward the south. Over a week later, having caught golden trout and climbed Mount Whitney, we followed him and so came to the great central camp at Monache Meadows.

Imagine an island-dotted lake of grass four or five miles long by two or three wide to which slope regular shores of stony soil planted with trees. Imagine on the very edge of that lake an especially fine grove perhaps a quarter of a mile in length, beneath whose trees a dozen different outfits of cowboys are camped for the summer. You must place a herd of ponies in the foreground, a pine mountain at the back, an unbroken ridge across ahead, cattle dotted here and there, thousands of ravens wheeling and croaking and flapping everywhere, a marvelous clear sun and blue sky. The camps were mostly open, though a few possessed tents. They differed from the ordinary in that they had racks for saddles and equipments. Especially well laid out were the cooking arrangements. A dozen accommodating springs supplied fresh water with the conveniently regular spacing of faucets.

Towards evening the men jingled in. This summer camp was almost in the nature of a vacation to them after the hard work of the desert. All they had to do was to ride about the pleasant hills examining that the cattle did not stray nor get into trouble. It was fun for them, and they were in high spirits.

Our immediate neighbors were an old man of seventy-two and his grandson of twenty-five. At least the old man said he was seventy-two. I should have guessed fifty. He was as straight as an arrow, wiry, lean, clear-eyed, and had, without food, ridden twelve hours after some strayed cattle. On arriving he threw off his saddle, turned his horse loose, and set about the construction of supper. This consisted of boiled meat, strong tea, and an incredible number of flapjacks built of water, baking-powder, salt, and flour, warmed through - not cooked - in a frying-pan. He deluged these with molasses and devoured three platefuls. It would have killed an ostrich, but apparently did this decrepit veteran of seventy-two much good.

After supper he talked to us most interestingly in the dry cowboy manner, looking at us keenly from under the floppy brim of his hat. He confided to us that he had had to quit smoking, and it ground him - he'd smoked since he was five years old.

"Tobacco doesn't agree with you any more?" I hazarded.

"Oh, 'taint that," he replied; "only I'd ruther chew."

The dark fell, and all the little camp-fires under the trees twinkled bravely forth. Some of the men sang. One had an accordion. Figures, indistinct and formless, wandered here and there in the shadows, suddenly emerging from mystery into the clarity of firelight, there to disclose themselves as visitors. Out on the plain the cattle lowed, the horses nickered. The red firelight flashed from the metal of suspended equipment, crimsoned the bronze of men's faces, touched with pink the high lights on their gracefully recumbent forms. After a while we rolled up in our blankets and went to sleep, while a band of coyotes wailed like lost spirits from a spot where a steer had died.

Stewart Edward White

XX

THE GOLDEN TROUT

After Farewell Gap, as has been hinted, the country changes utterly. Possibly that is why it is named Farewell Gap. The land is wild, weird, full of twisted trees, strangely colored rocks, fantastic formations, bleak mountains of slabs, volcanic cones, lava, dry powdery soil or loose shale, close-growing grasses, and strong winds. You feel yourself in an upper world beyond the normal, where only the freakish cold things of nature, elsewhere crowded out, find a home. Camp is under a lonely tree, none the less solitary from the fact that it has companions. The earth beneath is characteristic of the treeless lands, so that these seem to have been stuck alien into it. There is no shelter save behind great fortuitous rocks. Huge marmots run over the boulders, like little bears. The wind blows strong. The streams run naked under the eye of the sun, exposing clear and yellow every detail of their bottoms. In them there are no deep hiding-places any more than there is shelter in the land, and so every fish that swims shows as plainly as in an aquarium.

We saw them as we rode over the hot dry shale among the hot and twisted little trees. They lay against the bottom, transparent; they darted away from the jar of our horses' hoofs; they swam slowly against the current, delicate as liquid shadows, as though the clear uniform golden color of the bottom had clouded slightly to produce these tenuous ghostly forms. We examined them curiously from the advantage our slightly elevated trail gave us, and knew them for the Golden Trout, and longed to catch some.

All that day our route followed in general the windings of this unique home of a unique fish. We crossed a solid natural bridge; we skirted fields of red and black lava, vivid as poppies; we gazed marveling on perfect volcano cones, long since extinct: finally we camped on a side hill under two tall branchless trees in about as bleak and exposed a position as one could imagine. Then all three, we jointed our rods and went forth to find out what the Golden Trout was like.

I soon discovered a number of things, as follows: The stream at this point, near its source, is very narrow - I could step across it - and flows beneath deep banks. The Golden Trout is shy of approach. The wind blows. Combining these items of knowledge I found that it was no easy matter to cast forty feet in a high wind so accurately as to hit a three-foot stream a yard below the level of the ground. In fact, the proposition was distinctly sporty; I became as interested in it as in accurate target-shooting, so that at last I forgot utterly the intention of my efforts and failed to strike my first rise. The second, however, I hooked, and in a moment had him on the grass.

He was a little fellow of seven inches, but mere size was nothing, the color was the thing. And that was indeed golden. I can liken it to nothing more accurately than the twenty-dollar gold-piece, the same satin finish, the same pale yellow. The fish was fairly

Stewart Edward White

molten. It did not glitter in gaudy burnishment, as does our aquarium gold-fish, for example, but gleamed and melted and glowed as though fresh from the mould. One would almost expect that on cutting the flesh it would be found golden through all its substance. This for the basic color. You must remember always that it was a true trout, without scales, and so the more satiny. Furthermore, along either side of the belly ran two broad longitudinal stripes of exactly the color and burnish of the copper paint used on racing yachts.

I thought then, and have ever since, that the Golden Trout, fresh from the water, is one of the most beautiful fish that swims. Unfortunately it fades very quickly, and so specimens in alcohol can give no idea of it. In fact, I doubt if you will ever be able to gain a very clear idea of it unless you take to the trail that leads up, under the end of which is known technically as the High Sierras.

The Golden Trout lives only in this one stream, but occurs there in countless multitudes. Every little pool, depression, or riffles has its school. When not alarmed they take the fly readily. One afternoon I caught an even hundred in a little over an hour. By way of parenthesis it may be well to state that most were returned unharmed to the water. They run small, - a twelve-inch fish is a monster, - but are of extraordinary delicacy for eating. We three devoured sixty-five that first evening in camp.

Now the following considerations seem to me at this point worthy of note. In the first place, the Golden Trout occurs but in this one stream, and is easily caught. At present the stream is comparatively inaccessible, so that the natural supply probably keeps even with the season's catches. Still the trail is on the direct route to Mount Whitney, and year by year the ascent of this "top of the Republic" is becoming more the proper thing to do. Every camping party stops for a try at the Golden Trout, and of course the fish-hog is a sure occasional migrant. The cowboys told of two who caught six hundred in a day. As the certainly increasing tide of summer immigration gains in volume, the Golden Trout, in spite of his extraordinary numbers at present, is going to be caught out.

Therefore, it seems the manifest duty of the Fisheries to provide for the proper protection and distribution of this species, especially the distribution. Hundreds of streams in the Sierras are without trout simply because of some natural obstruction, such as a waterfall too high to jump, which prevents their ascent of the current. These are all well adapted to the planting of fish, and might just as well be stocked by the Golden Trout as by the customary Rainbow. Care should be taken lest the two species become hybridized, as has occurred following certain misguided efforts in the South Fork of the Kern.

So far as I know but one attempt has been made to transplant these fish. About five or six years ago a man named Grant carried some in pails across to a small lake near at hand. They have done well, and curiously enough have grown to a weight of from one and a half to two pounds. This would seem to show that their small size in Volcano Creek results entirely from conditions of feed or opportunity for development, and that a study of proper environment might result in a game fish to rival the Rainbow in size and certainly to surpass him in curious interest.

A great many well-meaning people who have marveled at the abundance of the Golden Trout in their natural habitat laugh at the idea that Volcano Creek will ever become "fished out." To such it should be pointed out that the fish in question is a voracious feeder, is without shelter, and quickly landed. A simple calculation will show how many fish a hundred moderate anglers, camping a week apiece, would take out in a season. And in a short time there will be many more than a hundred, few of them moderate, coming up into the mountains to camp just as long as they have a good time. All it needs is better trails, and better trails are under way. Well-meaning people used to laugh at the idea that the buffalo and wild pigeons would ever disappear. They are gone.

XXI

ON GOING OUT

The last few days of your stay in the wilderness you will be consumedly anxious to get out. It does not matter how much of a savage you are, how good a time you are having, or how long you have been away from civilization. Nor does it mean especially that you are glad to leave the wilds. Merely does it come about that you drift unconcernedly on the stream of days until you approach the brink of departure: then irresistibly the current hurries you into haste. The last day of your week's vacation; the last three of your month's or your summer's or your year's outing, - these comprise the hours in which by a mighty but invisible transformation your mind forsakes its savagery, epitomizes again the courses of social evolution, regains the poise and cultivation of the world of men. Before that you have been content; yes, and would have gone on being content for as long as you please until the approach of the limit you have set for your wandering.

In effect this transformation from the state of savagery to the state of civilization is very abrupt. When you leave the towns your clothes and mind are new. Only gradually do they take on the color of their environment; only gradually do the subtle influences of the great forest steal in on your dulled faculties to flow

Stewart Edward White

over them in a tide that rises imperceptibly. You glide as gently from the artificial to the natural life as do the forest shadows from night to day. But at the other end the affair is different. There you awake on the appointed morning in complete resumption of your old attitude of mind. The tide of nature has slipped away from you in the night.

Then you arise and do the most wonderful of your wilderness traveling. On those days you look back fondly, of them you boast afterwards in telling what a rapid and enduring voyager you are. The biggest day's journey I ever undertook was in just such a case. We started at four in the morning through a forest of the early spring-time, where the trees were glorious overhead, but the walking ankle deep. On our backs were thirty-pound burdens. We walked steadily until three in the afternoon, by which time we had covered thirty miles and had arrived at what then represented civilization to us. Of the nine who started, two Indians finished an hour ahead; the half breed, Billy, and I staggered in together, encouraging each other by words concerning the bottle of beer we were going to buy; and the five white men never got in at all until after nine o'clock that night. Neither thirty miles, nor thirty pounds, nor ankle-deep slush sounds formidable when considered as abstract and separate propositions.

In your first glimpse of the civilized peoples your appearance in your own eyes will undergo the same instantaneous and tremendous revulsion that has already taken place in your mental sphere. Heretofore you have considered yourself as a decently well appointed gentleman of the woods. Ten to one, in contrast to the voluntary or enforced simplicity of the professional woodsman you have looked on your little luxuries of carved leather hat-band, fancy knife sheath, pearl-handled six-shooter, or khaki breeches as giving you slightly the air of a forest exquisite. But on that depot platform or in presence of that staring group on the steps of the Pullman, you suddenly discover yourself to be nothing less than a disgrace to your bringing up. Nothing could be more evident than the flop of your hat, the faded, dusty appearance of your blue shirt, the beautiful black polish of your khakis, the grime of your knuckles, the three days' beard of your face. If you are a fool, you worry about it. If you are a sensible man, you do not mind; - and you prepare for amusing adventures.

The realization of your external unworthiness, however, brings to your heart the desire for a hot bath in a porcelain tub. You gloat over the thought; and when the dream comes to be a reality, you soak away in as voluptuous a pleasure as ever falls to the lot of man to enjoy. Then you shave, and array yourself minutely and preciously in clean clothes from head to toe, building up a new respectability, and you leave scornfully in a heap your camping garments. They have heretofore seemed clean, but now you would not touch them, no, not even to put them in the soiled-clothes basket, let your feminines rave as they may. And for at least two days you prove an almost childish delight in mere raiment.

But before you can reach this blissful stage you have still to order and enjoy your first civilized dinner. It tastes good, not because your camp dinners have palled on you, but because your transformation demands its proper aliment. Fortunate indeed you are if you step directly to a transcontinental train or into the streets of a modern town. Otherwise the transition through the small-hotel provender is apt to offer too little contrast for the fullest enjoyment. But aboard the dining-car or in the cafe you will gather to yourself such ill-assorted succulence as thick, juicy beefsteaks, and creamed macaroni, and sweet potatoes, and pie, and red wine, and real cigars and other things.

In their acquisition your appearance will tell against you. We were once watched anxiously by a nervous female head waiter who at last mustered up courage enough to inform me that guests were not allowed to eat without coats. We politely pointed out that we possessed no such garments. After a long consultation with the proprietor she told us it was all right for this time, but that we must not do it again. At another place I had to identify myself as a responsible person by showing a picture in a magazine bought for the purpose.

The public never will know how to take you. Most of it treats you as though you were a two-dollar a day laborer; some of the more astute are puzzled. One February I walked out of the North Country on snowshoes and stepped directly into a Canadian Pacific transcontinental train. I was clad in fur cap, vivid blanket coat, corded trousers, German stockings and moccasins; and my only baggage was the pair of snowshoes. It was the season of light travel. A single Englishman touring the world as the crow flies occupied the car. He looked at me so askance that I made an opportunity of talking to him. I should like to read his "Travels" to see what he made out of the riddle. In similar circumstances, and without explanation, I had fun talking French and swapping boulevard reminiscences with a member of a Parisian theatrical troupe making a long jump through northern

Wisconsin. And once, at six of the morning, letting myself into my own house with a latch-key, and sitting down to read the paper until the family awoke, I was nearly brained by the butler. He supposed me a belated burglar, and had armed himself with the poker. The most flattering experience of the kind was voiced by a small urchin who plucked at his mother's sleeve: "Look, mamma!" he exclaimed in guarded but jubilant tones, "there's a real Indian!"

Our last camp of this summer was built and broken in the full leisure of at least a three weeks' expectation. We had traveled south from the Golden Trout through the Toowah range. There we had viewed wonders which I cannot expect you to believe in, - such as a spring of warm water in which you could bathe and from which you could reach to dip up a cup of carbonated water on the right hand, or cast a fly into a trout stream, on the left. At length we entered a high meadow in the shape of a maltese cross, with pine slopes about it, and springs of water welling in little humps of green. There the long pine-needles were extraordinarily thick and the pine-cones exceptionally large. The former we scraped together to the depth of three feet for a bed in the lea of a fallen trunk; the latter we gathered in arm-fuls to pile on the camp-fire. Next morning we rode down a mile or so through the grasses, exclaimed over the thousands of mountain quail buzzing from the creek bottoms, gazed leisurely up at our well-known pines and about at the grateful coolness of our accustomed green meadows and leaves; - and then, as though we had crossed a threshold, we emerged into chaparral, dry loose shale, yucca, Spanish bayonet, heated air and the bleached burned-out furnace-like country of arid California in midsummer.

The trail dropped down through sage-brush, just as it always did in the California we had known; the mountains rose with the fur-like dark-olive effect of the coast ranges; the sun beat hot. We had left the enchanted land.

The trail was very steep and very long, and took us finally into the country of dry brown grasses, gray brush, waterless stony ravines, and dust. Others had traveled that trail, headed the other way, and evidently had not liked it. Empty bottles blazed the path. Somebody had sacrificed a pack of playing-cards, which he had stuck on thorns from time to time, each inscribed with a blasphemous comment on the discomforts of such travel. After an apparently interminable interval we crossed an irrigating ditch, where the horses were glad to water, and so came to one of those green flowering lush California villages so startlingly in contrast to their surroundings.

By this it was two o'clock and we had traveled on horseback since four. A variety of circumstances learned at the village made it imperative that both the Tenderfoot and myself should go out without the delay of a single hour. This left Wes to bring the horses home, which was tough on Wes, but he rose nobly to the occasion.

When the dust of our rustling cleared, we found we had acquired a team of wild broncos, a buckboard, an elderly gentleman with a white goatee, two bottles of beer, some crackers and some cheese. With these we hoped to reach the railroad shortly after midnight.

The elevation was five thousand feet, the road dusty and hot, the country uninteresting in sage-brush and alkali and rattlesnakes and general dryness. Constantly we drove, checking off the landmarks in the good old fashion. Our driver had immigrated from Maine the year before, and by some chance had drifted straight to the arid regions. He was vastly disgusted. At every particularly atrocious dust-hole or unlovely cactus strip he spat into space and remarked in tones of bottomless contempt: -

"BEAU-ti-ful Cal-if-or-nia!"

This was evidently intended as a quotation.

Towards sunset we ran up into rounded hills, where we got out at every rise in order to ease the horses, and where we hurried the old gentleman beyond the limits of his Easterner's caution at every descent.

It grew dark. Dimly the road showed gray in the twilight. We did not know how far exactly we were to go, but imagined that sooner or later we would top one of the small ridges to look across one of the broad plateau plains to the lights of our station. You see we had forgotten, in the midst of flatness, that we were still over five thousand feet up. Then the road felt its way between two hills; - and the blackness of night opened below us as well as above, and from some deep and tremendous abyss breathed the winds of space.

It was as dark as a cave, for the moon was yet two hours below the horizon. Somehow the trail turned to the right along that tremendous cliff. We thought we could make out its direction, the dimness of its glimmering; but equally well, after we had looked a moment, we could imagine it one way or another, to

Stewart Edward White

right and left. I went ahead to investigate. The trail to left proved to be the faint reflection of a clump of "old man" at least five hundred feet down; that to right was a burned patch sheer against the rise of the cliff. We started on the middle way.

There were turns-in where a continuance straight ahead would require an airship or a coroner; again turns-out where the direct line would telescope you against the state of California. These we could make out by straining our eyes. The horses plunged and snorted; the buckboard leaped. Fire flashed from the impact of steel against rock, momentarily blinding us to what we should see. Always we descended into the velvet blackness of the abyss, the canon walls rising steadily above us shutting out even the dim illumination of the stars. From time to time our driver, desperately scared, jerked out cheering bits of information.

"My eyes ain't what they was. For the Lord's sake keep a-lookin', boys."

"That nigh hoss is deef. There don't seem to be no use saying WHOA to her."

"Them brakes don't hold fer sour peanuts. I been figgerin' on tackin' on a new shoe for a week."

"I never was over this road but onct, and then I was headed th' other way. I was driving of a corpse."

Then, after two hours of it, BING! BANG! SMASH! our tongue collided with a sheer black wall, no blacker than the atmosphere before it. The trail here took a sharp V turn to the left. We had left the face of the precipice and henceforward would descend the bed of the canon. Fortunately our collision had done damage to nothing but our nerves, so we proceeded to do so.

The walls of the crevice rose thousands of feet above us. They seemed to close together, like the sides of a tent, to leave only a narrow pale lucent strip of sky. The trail was quite invisible, and even the sense of its existence was lost when we traversed groves of trees. One of us had to run ahead of the horses, determining its general direction, locating the sharper turns. The rest depended on the instinct of the horses and pure luck.

It was pleasant in the cool of night thus to run down through the blackness, shouting aloud to guide our followers, swinging to the slope, bathed to the soul in mysteries of which we had no time to take cognizance.

By and by we saw a little spark far ahead of us like a star. The smell of fresh wood smoke and stale damp fire came to our nostrils. We gained the star and found it to be a log smouldering; and up the hill other stars red as blood. So we knew that we had crossed the zone of an almost extinct forest fire,
and looked on the scattered camp-fires of an army
of destruction.

The moon rose. We knew it by touches of white light on peaks infinitely far above us; not at all by the relieving of the heavy velvet blackness in which we moved. After a time, I, running ahead in my turn, became aware of the deep breathing of animals. I stopped short and called a warning. Immediately a voice answered me.

"Come on, straight ahead. They're not on the road."

When within five feet I made out the huge freight wagons in which were lying the teamsters, and very dimly the big freight mules standing tethered to the wheels.

"It's a dark night, friend, and you're out late."

"A dark night," I agreed, and plunged on. Behind me rattled and banged the abused buckboard, snorted the half-wild broncos, groaned the unrepaired brake, softly cursed my companions.

Then at once the abrupt descent ceased. We glided out to the silvered flat, above which sailed the moon.

The hour was seen to be half past one. We had missed our train. Nothing was visible of human habitations. The land was frosted with the moonlight, enchanted by it, etherealized. Behind us, huge and formidable, loomed the black mass of the range we had descended. Before us, thin as smoke in the magic lucence that flooded the world, rose other mountains, very great, lofty as the sky. We could not understand them. The descent we had just accomplished should have landed us on a level plain in which lay our town. But here we found ourselves in a pocket valley entirely surrounded by mountain ranges through which there seemed to be no pass less than five or six thousand feet in height.

We reined in the horses to figure it out.

"I don't see how it can be," said I. "We've certainly come far enough. It would take us four hours at the very least to cross that range, even if the railroad should happen to be on the other side of it."

"I been through here only once," repeated the driver, - "going the other way. - Then I drew a corpse." He spat, and added as an afterthought, "BEAU-ti-ful Cal-if-or-nia!"

We stared at the mountains that hemmed us in. They rose above us sheer and forbidding. In the bright moonlight plainly were to be descried the brush of the foothills, the timber, the fissures, the canons, the granites, and the everlasting snows. Almost we thought to make out a thread of a waterfall high up where the clouds would be if the night had not been clear.

"We got off the trail somewhere," hazarded the Tenderfoot.

"Well, we're on a road, anyway," I pointed out. "It's bound to go somewhere. We might as well give up the railroad and find a place to turn-in."

"It can't be far," encouraged the Tenderfoot; "this valley can't be more than a few miles across."

"Gi dap!" remarked the driver.

We moved forward down the white wagon trail approaching the mountains. And then we were witnesses of the most marvelous transformation. For as we neared them, those impregnable mountains, as though panic-stricken by our advance, shrunk back, dissolved, dwindled, went to pieces. Where had towered ten-thousand-foot peaks, perfect in the regular succession from timber to snow, now were little flat hills on which grew tiny bushes of sage. A passage opened between them. In a hundred yards we had gained the open country, leaving behind us the mighty but unreal necromancies of the moon.

Before us gleamed red and green lights. The mass of houses showed half distinguishable. A feeble glimmer illuminated part of a white sign above the depot. That which remained invisible was evidently the name of the town. That which was revealed was the supplementary information which the Southern Pacific furnishes to its patrons. It read: "Elevation 482 feet." We were definitely out of the mountains.

XXII

THE LURE OF THE TRAIL

The trail's call depends not at all on your common sense. You know you are a fool for answering it; and yet you go. The comforts of civilization, to put the case on its lowest plane, are not lightly to be renounced: the ease of having your physical labor done for you; the joy of cultivated minds, of theatres, of books, of participation in the world's progress; these you leave behind you. And in exchange you enter a life where there is much long hard work of the hands - work that is really hard and long, so that no man paid to labor would consider it for a moment; you undertake to eat simply, to endure much, to lie on the rack of anxiety; you voluntarily place yourself where cold, wet, hunger, thirst, heat, monotony, danger, and many discomforts will wait upon you daily. A thousand times in the course of a woods life even the stoutest-hearted will tell himself softly - very softly if he is really stout-hearted, so that others may not be annoyed - that if ever the fates permit him to extricate himself he will never venture again.

These times come when long continuance has worn on the spirit. You beat all day to windward against the tide toward what should be but an hour's sail: the sea is high and the spray cold; there are sunken rocks, and food there is none; chill gray evening draws dangerously near, and there is a foot of water in the bilge. You have swallowed your tongue twenty times on the alkali; and the sun is melting hot, and the dust dry and pervasive, and there is no water, and for all your effort the relative distances seem to remain the same for days. You have carried a pack until your every muscle is strung white-hot; the woods are breathless; the black flies swarm persistently and bite until your face is covered with blood. You have struggled through clogging snow until each time you raise your snowshoe you feel as though some one had stabbed a little sharp knife into your groin; it has come to be night; the mercury is away below zero, and with aching fingers you are to prepare a camp which is only an anticipation of many more such camps in the ensuing days. For a week it has rained, so that you, pushing through the dripping brush, are soaked and sodden and comfortless, and the bushes have become horrible to your shrinking goose-flesh. Or you are just plain tired out, not from a single day's fatigue, but from the gradual exhaustion of a long hike. Then in your secret soul you utter these sentiments: -

"You are a fool. This is not fun. There is no real reason why you should do this. If you ever get out of here, you will stick right home where common sense flourishes, my son!"

Then after a time you do get out, and are thankful. But in three months you will have proved in your own experience the following axiom - I should call it the widest truth the wilderness has to teach: -

"In memory the pleasures of a camping trip strengthen with time, and the disagreeables weaken."

I don't care how hard an experience you have had, nor how little of the pleasant has been mingled with it, in three months your general impression of that trip will be good. You will look back on the hard times with a certain fondness of recollection.

I remember one trip I took in the early spring following a long drive on the Pine River. It rained steadily for six days. We were soaked to the skin all the time, ate standing up in the driving downpour, and slept wet. So cold was it that each morning our blankets were so full of frost that they crackled stiffly when we turned out. Dispassionately I can appraise that as about the worst I ever got into. Yet as an impression the Pine River trip seems to me a most enjoyable one.

So after you have been home for a little while the call begins to make itself heard. At first it is very gentle. But little by little a restlessness seizes hold of you. You do not know exactly what is the matter: you are aware merely that your customary life has lost savor, that you are doing things more or less perfunctorily, and that you are a little more irritable than your naturally evil disposition.

And gradually it is borne in on you exactly what is the matter. Then say you to yourself: -

"My son, you know better. You are no tenderfoot. You have had too long an experience to admit of any glamour of indefiniteness about this thing. No use bluffing. You know exactly how hard you will have to work, and how much tribulation you are going to get into, and how hungry and wet and cold and tired and generally frazzled out you are going to be. You've been there enough times so it's pretty clearly impressed on you. You go into this thing with your eyes open. You know what you're in for. You're pretty well off right here, and you'd be a fool to go."

"That's right," says yourself to you. "You're dead right about it, old man. Do you know where we can get another pack-mule?"

Choose from Thousands of 1stWorldLibrary Classics By

Adolphus WilliamWard
Aesop
Agatha Christie
Alexander Aaronsohn
Alexander Kielland
Alexandre Dumas
Alfred Gatty
Alfred Ollivant
Alice Duer Miller
Alice Turner Curtis
Alice Dunbar
Ambrose Bierce
Amelia E. Barr
Andrew Lang
Andrew McFarland Davis
Anna Sewell
Annie Besant
Annie Hamilton Donnell
Annie Payson Call
Anton Chekhov
Arnold Bennett
Arthur Conan Doyle
Arthur Ransome
Atticus
B. M. Bower
Basil King
Bayard Taylor
Ben Macomber
Booth Tarkington
Bram Stoker
C. Collodi
C. E. Orr
C. M. Ingleby
Carolyn Wells
Catherine Parr Traill
Charles A. Eastman
Charles Dickens
Charles Dudley Warner
Charles Farrar Browne
Charles Ives
Charles Kingsley
Charles Lathrop Pack
Charles Whibley
Charles Willing Beale
Charlotte M. Braeme
Charlotte M.Yonge
Clair W. Hayes
Clarence Day Jr.
Clarence E. Mulford

Clemence Housman
Confucius
Cornelis DeWitt Wilcox
Cyril Burleigh
D. H. Lawrence
Daniel Defoe
David Garnett
Don Carlos Janes
Donald Keyhole
Dorothy Kilner
Dougan Clark
E. Nesbit
E.P.Roe
E. Phillips Oppenheim
Edgar Allan Poe
Edgar Rice Burroughs
Edith Wharton
Edward J. O'Biren
John Cournos
Edwin L. Arnold
Eleanor Atkins
Elizabeth Cleghorn
Gaskell
Elizabeth Von Arnim
Ellem Key
Emily Dickinson
Erasmus W. Jones
Ernie Howard Pie
Ethel Turner
Ethel Watts Mumford
Eugenie Foa
Eugene Wood
Evelyn Everett-Green
Everard Cotes
F. J. Cross
Federick Austin Ogg
Ferdinand Ossendowski
Francis Bacon
Francis Darwin
Frances Hodgson Burnett
Frank Gee Patchin
Frank Harris
Frank Jewett Mather
Frank L. Packard
Frederick Trevor Hill
Frederick Winslow Taylor
Friedrich Kerst
Friedrich Nietzsche
Fyodor Dostoyevsky

Gabrielle E. Jackson
Garrett P. Serviss
Gaston Leroux
George Ade
Geroge Bernard Shaw
George Ebers
George Eliot
George MacDonald
George Orwell
George Tucker
George W. Cable
George Wharton James
Gertrude Atherton
Grace E. King
Grant Allen
Guillermo A. Sherwell
Gulielma Zollinger
Gustav Flaubert
H. A. Cody
H. B. Irving
H. G. Wells
H. H. Munro
H. Irving Hancock
H. Rider Haggard
H. W. C. Davis
Hamilton Wright Mabie
Hans Christian Andersen
Harold Avery
Harold McGrath
Harriet Beecher Stowe
Harry Houidini
Helent Hunt Jackson
Helen Nicolay
Hendy David Thoreau
Henrik Ibsen
Henry Adams
Henry Ford
Henry Frost
Henry James
Henry Jones Ford
Henry Seton Merriman
Henry Wadsworth
Longfellow
Henry W Longfellow
Herbert A. Giles
Herbert N. Casson
Herman Hesse
Homer
Honore De Balzac

Horace Walpole
Horatio Alger, Jr.
Howard Pyle
Howard R. Garis
Hugh Lofting
Hugh Walpole
Humphry Ward
Ian Maclaren
Israel Abrahams
J.G.Austin
J. Henri Fabre
J. M. Barrie
J. Macdonald Oxley
J. S. Knowles
J. Storer Clouston
Jack London
Jacob Abbott
James Allen
James Lane Allen
James Andrews
James Baldwin
James DeMille
James Joyce
James Oliver Curwood
James Oppenheim
James Otis
Jane Austen
Jens Peter Jacobsen
Jerome K. Jerome
John Burroughs
John F. Kennedy
John Gay
John Glasworthy
John Habberton
John Joy Bell
John Milton
John Philip Sousa
Jonathan Swift
Joseph Carey
Joseph Conrad
Joseph Jacobs
Julian Hawthrone
Julies Vernes
Justin Huntly McCarthy
Kakuzo Okakura
Kenneth Grahame
Kate Langley Bosher
L. A. Abbot
L. T. Meade
L. Frank Baum
Laura Lee Hope

Laurence Housman
Leo Tolstoy
Leonid Andreyev
Lewis Carroll
Lilian Bell
Lloyd Osbourne
Louis Tracy
Louisa May Alcott
Lucy Fitch Perkins
Lucy Maud Montgomery
Lydia Miller Middleton
Lyndon Orr
M. H. Adams
Margaret E. Sangster
Margaret Vandercook
Maria Edgeworth
Maria Thompson Daviess
Mariano Azuela
Marion Polk Angellotti
Mark Overton
Mark Twain
Mary Austin
Mary Cole
Mary Rowlandson
Mary Wollstonecraft
Shelley
Max Beerbohm
Myra Kelly
Nathaniel Hawthrone
O. F. Walton
Oscar Wilde
Owen Johnson
P.G.Wodehouse
Paul and Mable Thorn
Paul G. Tomlinson
Paul Severing
Peter B. Kyne
Plato
R. Derby Holmes
R. L. Stevenson
Rabindranath Tagore
Rahul Alvares
Ralph Waldo Emmerson
Rene Descartes
Rex E. Beach
Richard Harding Davis
Richard Jefferies
Robert Barr
Robert Frost
Robert Gordon Anderson
Robert L. Drake

Robert Lansing
Robert Michael Ballantyne
Robert W. Chambers
Rosa Nouchette Carey
Ross Kay
Rudyard Kipling
Samuel B. Allison
Samuel Hopkins Adams
Sarah Bernhardt
Selma Lagerlof
Sherwood Anderson
Sigmund Freud
Standish O'Grady
Stanley Weyman
Stella Benson
Stephen Crane
Stewart Edward White
Stijn Streuvels
Swami Abhedananda
Swami Parmananda
T. S. Ackland
The Princess Der Ling
Thomas A. Janvier
Thomas A Kempis
Thomas Anderton
Thomas Bailey Aldrich
Thomas Bulfinch
Thomas De Quincey
Thomas H. Huxley
Thomas Hardy
Thomas More
Thornton W. Burgess
U. S. Grant
Valentine Williams
Victor Appleton
Virginia Woolf
Walter Scott
Washington Irving
Wilbur Lawton
Wilkie Collins
Willa Cather
Willard F. Baker
William Makepeace
Thackeray
William W. Walter
Winston Churchill
Yei Theodora Ozaki
Young E. Allison
Zane Grey